The Guardians: **War Zone**

Richard Austin is the pseudonym of a popular

science fiction adventure writer.

Also by Richard Austin in Pan Books

THE GUARDIANS
THE GUARDIANS: *Trial by Fire*
THE GUARDIANS: *Thunder of Hell*
THE GUARDIANS: *Night of the Phoenix*
THE GUARDIANS: *Armageddon Run*

Richard Austin

THE GUARDIANS
WAR ZONE

PAN BOOKS
London, Sydney and Auckland

First published 1986 by Jove Books, a division of
the Berkley Publishing Group, New York

This edition published 1990 by Pan Books Ltd,
Cavaye Place, London SW10 9PG

9 8 7 6 5 4 3 2 1

ISBN 0 330 31663 X

Printed in England by Clays Ltd, St Ives plc

Acknowledgements:
Thanks to Robert Pruden and John Brooks
for advice and technical information

For Julie,
the skeptic

PROLOGUE

All roads led to Washington, and all roads were hell.

The Guardians—Billy McKay, Sam Sloan, Tom Rogers, Casey Wilson—had just touched down on the last leg of their nightmare odyssey across enemy-occupied America. They had one thought in mind as they drove from the wreckage of the shattered C-130 that had carried them from New Mexico: to get President of the United States Jeffrey MacGregor safely into the White House before the legions of the FSE Expeditionary Force closed in.

It took them until full dark to get to the outskirts of D.C. And if the roads were hell, what they met when they crossed the Beltway . . .

Stalled cars in profusion; go around or bulldoze through. Streets choked with rubble so deep the straining armored car could barely scale the mounds, treacherous ground that threatened to swallow them with every meter. Blocks of burned-out buildings as lush

1

in wreckage as the Amazon Basin was in greenery.

And the people, denizens of the blackest pit of hell. Glimpses now and again of forms flitting through ruins, staring from cavern storefronts, gazing down from rooftops. Many shouted obscenities, hurled rocks and bottles impotently against the steel-and-titanium hide of Mobile One. Occasional shots flashed from the dark and ricocheted harmlessly off the hull; once, a rocket fired from a third story etched a line of sparks right in front of the car's nose. Tom Rogers hosed the front of the building it had come from with lead and white phosphorus death. A shrieking, blazing figure staggered out of the tentacles of white smoke, pitched into a pile of rubble, and lay thrashing. They drove on.

Once a mob confronted them, shouting angry faces, hands and boards and bits of rubble pounding on the hull. Torches waved like banners of flame; the occupants of the car looked in all directions for the orange meteor of a Molotov coming their way.

They weren't disappointed. McKay was looking out the portside viewslit when a gasoline bomb arced in from the left and behind, splashing right below the firing port. McKay jerked back reflexively with a curse. "Goose her, Case, get us out of here!"

Casey cast one bleak look back at McKay. There were dozens of people crowded in front of them, pressed together solidly against the car.

McKay chanced another glance outside the port. A filter of fire danced before his eyes. There didn't seem to be any way it was going to get inside, though he sure as hell wasn't going to stick his head out to check unless it became absolutely necessary. But he would take no chances with the President's life—not with their goal practically in sight.

"Casey—go for it!" Casey gulped and hit the accelerator.

People screamed as their bodies squashed beneath the tires of the mammoth car. McKay heard a thump, a bang, a hissing explosion as Tom Rogers unloaded a CS hand grenade out the top hatch of the turret. That thinned the crowd away some. Then Rogers let loose a long ripping burst over their heads from the turret guns and the mob fled in all directions. Casey sped ahead.

Through the long, hot, deadly night they drove. And then they were slanting down New York Avenue, miraculously clear of cars and rubble, between the Treasury and the Treasury Annex, and there were figures stirring sleepily around guttering campfires among bare trees in Lafayette Park, and on the left . . .

Battered and blackened, collapsed in places, but still miraculously intact: the White House. McKay gripped Casey's shoulder. "Go for it! Hit it hard!"

A muzzle flash blossomed from the darkness of the park, then another, then a ragged volley of full-auto fire rippling across a handful of single shots. Rogers's M-19 boomed in response. Grenades made fire fountains of the trampled mud, which had once been pampered turf.

Brakes locked, the car skidded to a halt before the main entrance. Even McKay appreciated the irony; the last time they had seen this battered portico had been under similar circumstances—hunkered down and taking fire as the mobs attacked after the all-clear sounded.

Tom Rogers returned fire among the trees of the North Lawn while Casey turned the car around in its tracks so McKay and Sloan, supporting the President between them, could bail out the side. They ran up the steps of the White House, a bewildered Dr. Srinarampa trotting at their heels, McKay blazing into the night one-

handed with his M-60 machine gun, Sloan humping his Galil-203 combo.

Bullets cracked about them, throwing stinging sprays of marble chips into their hands and faces, and then they were into the entranceway, where year-old skeletons still sprawled on the faded, water-stained carpet. Casey goosed the vehicle through another one-eighty and dived for the new subterranean-garage exit that led in under the West Wing, so that Tom Rogers could fire up the snipers from a hull-down position.

Inside, the building was deserted, empty. There was no sign of life anywhere, inside or on the North or South Lawns. It was as if the gangs that warred for control of the wreckage of Washington had, by mutual unspoken agreement, decided the grounds were sacrosanct. As Sam Sloan hustled the President to relative safety downstairs, McKay tore through closet storage on the ground floor in a frantic search. In a matter of moments he found what he was looking for, dashed for the stairs.

A hailstorm of gunfire greeted McKay's solitary figure as it emerged on the third-floor promenade. Ignoring the shots ricocheting all around, he moved to the center of the facade, hurriedly but purposefully. The shooters out in the park redoubled their efforts.

Then, as dawn filled the eastern horizon, the first sunlight of the Fourth of July fell across the flag of the United States as it unfurled from the White House flagpole. The snipers ceased their barrage, momentarily awestruck as they saw the flag of their country flying from that spot for the first time in over a year.

McKay stood beside it, proud in his brief moment of emotional defiance. For him, America . . . had come home.

CHAPTER
ONE ──────────────────

For a moment that seemed to stretch for an eternity, the flag flapped in the early dawn light. Then from among the trees of Lafayette Park a single shot cracked. There was a vicious little *pop* and the flag jerked as a bullet hole appeared in its center.

"Well, it was fun while it lasted," Billy McKay said, sticking his last cigar in his mouth and striking a match.

The gunshot was a real show opener. It had scarcely finished reverberating among the ruins of downtown Washington when a fierce fusillade of fire ripped out of the park. McKay made himself very small behind the parapet as clouds of plaster dust billowed up around him. Pieces of the few slates remaining on the roof of the North Portico rained down on him as he poked his M-60E3 over the edge of the roofline and cut loose with a burst. At once the firing slacked; whoever the bad guys were, they didn't seem to have automatic weapons, and didn't seem any too eager to face up to automatic fire in return.

"McKay?" It was Sam Sloan's voice, coming through the bone-conduction speaker taped to the mastoid process behind McKay's ear. "Are you all right up there?"

McKay peered through the feeble dawn light. Beyond the spike-tipped, black wrought-iron fence, its gates trampled down by a furious mob on War Day over a year ago but otherwise surprisingly intact, he could see figures moving through the undergrowth that now crowded the trees in the park. "Affirmative, for now. But those bastards are liable to get bold when they realize how few of us are in here."

"Want me to come up and lend a hand?" Sloan asked.

McKay whipped the buttstock of his chopped-down machine gun to his shoulder, holding it by fore and rear pistol grips like a gigantic Tommy gun, and ripped off a short burst. Across the street a figure exploded out of a bush backwards, a long black M-16 rifle dropping from his hands. *So they got autoweapons after all,* he thought. *Unless that's a civilian model.* "Stay down there and keep an eye on the President," he replied.

"What about the Ellipse, Billy?" drawled the soft voice of Tom Rogers. He was sitting behind the two big guns in Mobile One's turret, hull-down in the entrance to the subterranean garage beneath the West Wing.

"Aw, shit." He had one bitch of a tactical problem facing him. One not even the fantastically intensive Guardians training had covered. Billy McKay was a maximum marine, a beer-guzzling brawler who preferred, when all was said and done, to let his balls or his sledgehammer fists do his thinking for him. But he wasn't commander of the Guardians, the most elite military team ever assembled, for nothing; his close-cropped blond head wasn't bone all the way through, no matter what Sam Sloan affected to believe.

"Cancel that. Sloan, hustle your butt up here with your Galil-203. Case, shift on up to the turret and cover the North Lawn. Tom, set up some Claymores up front and around the entrances, in case our buddies get any bright ideas. Mr. President—" He paused. Giving orders to the Commander in Chief was not easy for a man whose highest rank had been first lieutenant, and who still thought of himself as a sergeant.

"Go ahead, McKay. I'm at your command," came the calm voice of Jeffrey MacGregor, now the youngest President ever to occupy the White House.

McKay's head nodded on its thick neck. MacGregor had some mushy liberal notions, but when it came to the crunch, he was all right. "Mr. President, hole up in one of the rooms off the foyer with a CAWS and shoot anything that tries to come through the door unless you know it's one of us. Can you get Dr. S to lend a hand?" With all the grief he had, McKay refused to try to pronounce the name of the Indian-born doctor, one of the far-flung participants of the Blueprint for Renewal who'd been handed to them by their allies back in Albuquerque, New Mexico.

"I'm afraid not," MacGregor said. "He refuses to touch any weapons."

Squinting over the parapet of the promenade, McKay scowled. Given that the Guardians' primary mission had always been to protect the President, it really griped him to leave MacGregor on his own down there. But the best way of ensuring his security was to make sure no bad guys got into shooting range of him, and that required the use of his desperately few warm bodies to secure the area as best as could be done.

Besides, MacGregor wasn't exactly helpless; more than once during the past year he'd fought—not unwillingly—in his own defense, and the super 12-gauge Close Assault Weapons System they'd given him would make him a very formidable foe indeed if anybody did manage to get in the room with him.

The Guardians acknowledged their commander's orders and set about carrying them out with calm efficiency, as if this were something they did every day of their lives, securing as much as possible of the sprawling White House complex against what might well be a whole city full of unseen enemies.

In a moment McKay heard the sputter of a small-caliber weapon close behind him. "Sam? Is that you?" His chilly blue eyes never left off scanning the trees.

"Affirmative, McKay. We've got some company down on the Ellipse."

"How many?"

"Not many, looks like. Looks like they're trying to infiltrate people back there, to hem us in."

For a while that was all that happened. A few shots came cracking out of Lafayette Park, or up from the Ellipse. People continued to try to slip into the mostly bare park south of the White House. While not the master sniper Casey Wilson was, Sloan had a keen eye and a steady hand and benefit of the world's most intensive marksmanship training. He picked off several forms slipping furtively into the bedraggled trees of the South Lawn. He could have knocked down more, but he'd never had any stomach for killing. Those he shot, he did so by way of discouraging their fellows, hoping to save lives in the long run.

At McKay's orders he didn't make use of the stubby 40-millimeter grenade launcher affixed under his Galil assault rifle's barrel. The burly ex-marine had decided that the benefits of not giving away too much information about their capabilities outweighed the chance that their enemies—whoever they were—would give up and go away rather than face the weapon. Hell, the sons of bitches hadn't been discouraged by Mobile One's armament, which consisted of a grenade launcher a lot more powerful than Sloan's single-shot job, and fully automatic to boot, and a Browning M-2 .50-caliber machine gun that could shoot through a locomotive.

Even though a lot of the trees on and near the White House grounds had been scorched by the thermal flashes of exploding hydrogen warheads, the intensive rain that had followed the One-Day War over most of the North American continent had brought out the undergrowth in lush profusion. The ceremonial shrubs had run amok, providing a good deal of cover to Tom Rogers as he set his nasty little command-detonated mines to cover the approaches to the structure. Nevertheless, from time to time a few rounds came his way, and Billy McKay's M-60 blazed angry response. In time, the ex-Green Beret reported he was done.

"Right," McKay replied. "Take over the turret again. Case, you go inside and keep an eye on the President. Sloan, go down and start scoping the place out. I want to know what kind of resources we got."

"But McKay—"

"Move out, Sloan."

"What about your back, Billy?" Casey Wilson asked, his Southern California voice as mellow as always.

"Send Dr. S up here. Maybe he can't use no gun, but does his religion say that he can't play lookout?"

Sloan went below. In a moment Dr. Srinarampa turned up, shy and apologetic, to ask McKay where he wanted him to go. The chubby little doctor showed no sign of alarm at the occasional bullet that cracked overhead. "Go around and take up position in the Sun Room," McKay told him. "And keep your fuckin' head *down*."

New dispositions made, McKay settled down for another spell of waiting. This was always the hardest part of battle for him—the long, inevitable gaps in the action, where nothing happened, but you didn't dare relax for one single sliver of a second. It was time tailor-made for fretting.

And Billy McKay had a lot to fret about. For one thing, he and his men had been virtually without rest for the fifty most harrowing hours they'd known in their far-from-settled lives. And even before that they'd had little enough rest—a few hours snatched on the air mattresses in Mobile One before rolling up to the gates of Kirtland Air Force Base in New Mexico, making use of the ultrasecret codes and recognition sequences they'd captured with the vehicle to pose as Federated States of Europe Expeditionary Force wheels on some super-classified assignment to bluff their way inside. There had been the quick, briefly vicious struggle to secure the base from its Effsee garrison, with the help of Kirtland's original complement, which the interlopers had believed thoroughly cowed. And then, without a chance to rest, they'd been bundled aboard the big C-130 transport plane the grateful Kirtland personnel provided to whisk them across the hostile continent to the place they had decided would be the new safe haven from which President MacGregor would try to reestablish his control over a shattered America.

That had seemed too good to be true. It *had* been. The Effsees had been alert and angry; the Guardians had snatched MacGregor out of the Expeditionary Force-occupied Heartland complex in the center of Iowa, destroying the facility, the records of Project

Blueprint, and almost the entirety of the Expeditionary Force high command. In the past few weeks they and the President had slipped through the Effsees' fingers time and again. Though comparatively small, the Expeditionary Force ruled the skies over North America, and when their forces on the Eastern Seaboard detected the approach of an aircraft that wasn't one of theirs, they reacted with the whipcrack ferocity of a rattlesnake.

An F-15 Eagle had been scrambled to shoot the unknown aircraft down. Between the big, fast, powerful fighter and the lumbering, prop-driven Hercules there should have been no contest: one firing pass with missiles and 20-millimeter Gatling, and a cruciform pyre blazing on the ground. But at the controls of the lumbering Herkie had been Casey Wilson, the finest combat pilot America had ever produced.

What happened instead was a bizarre battle among the skyscrapers of downtown Baltimore, Casey whipping his huge craft around as if it were a fighter, actually dodging between buildings—an environment where the Eagle's terrific speed acted against it. Though the Hercules had taken terrific punishment and almost its entire crew had been killed, Casey'd managed to hang on until the F-15 driver got so furious he made a long dive through cloud cover—in pursuit of what he thought was his helplessly stricken prey—right smack into the side of a building.

Casey fought the big bird to a landing outside the capital, and for all that night they'd battled their way through the gang-infested rubble of Washington, driving like mad things to reach their goal: the White House. They didn't know if they could secure it, they didn't know if they could hold it, they didn't even know if it was still standing. But each of them knew that of all the places from which America's rebuilding could be directed, the tremendous symbolic significance of the White House made it the best choice.

Now they were here. And McKay was beginning to wonder if it had been such a hot idea.

As far as he or any of them knew, they were cut off totally from food, water, and any kind of outside support. There were bad guys all around them.

While the big Cadillac Gage V-450 Super Commando they'd stolen out of Heartland to replace their original, lost Mobile One was crammed to the gills with enough ammunition to fight the young war they now seemed to be facing, ammunition wasn't the real issue. It was the sheer paucity of defenders. Supersoldiers though they were, there was no way that the Guardians were going to hang on to the White House indefinitely against any type of determined enemy. They were smart, brave, and trained as no one had ever been trained. But they weren't bulletproof.

There was also the problem of resupply. Just the six of them could go through an awful lot of food and water—especially water—mighty quickly. And looters weren't liable to have left a lot in the cupboards.

The decision to come to Washington had been emotional as much as reasonable. It had only been reached after the other logical places to settle down—Kansas City, the Denver Federal Center, someplace in California—had proven to be unacceptable. The Guardians and MacGregor had had faith that they could make the Washington move work. *If* they could, there was no question it was the best.

But could they hold? They'd known there was risk, known they were initially going to be cut off from food and water, fuel for the emergency generators to provide power. They did not realize they would find themselves instantly besieged. They'd expected at least some leeway, a time to get set up, time even to send out feelers to whoever else lived in the rubble.

But there'd been no time to talk. Everybody they'd seen since hitting the outskirts of D.C. had been out to do them harm.

"McKay."

"Yeah, Sam?" The sun was almost overhead, and the humid air didn't give McKay's sweat-soaked back and shoulders a chance to dry. He wiped sweat from his eyes. He hadn't seen any motion for almost half an hour, but his eyes never quit scanning the trees of Lafayette Park.

"It's the damnedest thing, McKay," said Sloan. "You'll remember when we pulled out we left a lot of stores behind—a year's supply of food for a couple dozen people, medical supplies, stored water, even weapons and ammunition and vehicles in the lockers in the underground garage."

"Affirmative. So?"

"So it's still here. All of it, from the boxes of Quaker Oats sitting on the shelves in unlocked pantries to the top-secret electronics equipment down below."

"How'd you find that out?" When they'd gone underground, on that first, horrible day when the crowd was coming over the wire, they'd thrown a switch that arc-welded shut the massive metal door leading to the underground area.

"Tom took a break from the turret while I spelled him and blew down the emergency door. Since we were hoping to use this place as a full-scale national headquarters, I wanted to know if by chance some of the equipment survived. And all of it did. *All* of it."

"You mean there's nothing missing?"

"Not that I can find. The technicians who pulled out

after we left cleared out their lockers, and took some of the more obviously valuable and portable equipment with them. Other than that . . . nothing. Even the bodies of the rioters we killed—skeletons—are lying where they fell, with their weapons beside them.''

"Jesus Christ." From the way that mob had come on, he was mildly surprised that they left anything standing above ground level. For them not even to police up the weapons of their fallen comrades—it was a mystery. McKay hated mysteries.

"Tom? Casey? You make anything of this?''

"Beats me, man.''

"Sounds as if somebody got to the rioters almost as soon as we pulled out,'' Tom Rogers said. "And like somebody's been keeping people away ever since. Maybe the same somebody.'' For Rogers it was a lengthy speech.

"Who'd do that?'' Casey asked.

"And why?'' Sloan added.

"If that's so, why ain't they here to greet us?'' McKay demanded. It was one of the few times he ever could remember taking issue with Rogers. When that stocky, soft-spoken soldier up and said something, it generally made solid sense.

But Rogers had nothing more to say, so that's all he said. Casey and Sloan, the theoreticians of the group, had begun to talk over one another, spilling out suggestions, hypotheses, and objections, when Dr. Srinarampa's voice hesitantly called, "Please hurry, come and look. They are coming now, yes.''

CHAPTER
TWO ――――――――――――――

"I see 'em, Billy!" yelled Casey Wilson, looking out over the South Lawn from the ruins of the Blue Room, off toward the Ellipse with the stump of the fallen Washington Monument in the background.

"Get back in One and get ready to drive," McKay rapped. "Sam, get up top and take over for the doctor. Tom, if you see anything coming down from the north, fire it up without even *asking*."

Again he swept the park with his eyes, then made a lightning decision. He pushed back from the balustrade, picked up his machine gun and dodged into an open doorway yawning behind him. Shots from a couple of alert enemies cracked the facade as he disappeared inside. He dodged through staff quarters and guest rooms thick with the smells of mildew and decay, racing into the Sun Room on the south side to find the doctor hunkered down, staring round-eyed as a dozen men dashed across the street and scaled the fence surrounding the grounds.

McKay leaped over the low sill of a window long since denuded of glass and threw himself face-down on the promenade. Fortunately a year's weather had sluiced away the razor shards of broken glass. He poked the M-60's muzzle up through the marble railing, swept a belt of ammunition off one shoulder, and fired a quick burst.

The opposition had come out of the scrub in a sort of semicircle up from where East and West Executive Avenues met at the Zero Milestone, keeping well separated. That wasn't so good; it looked like they'd encountered automatic weapons before, had some idea how to cope with them, and wouldn't obligingly freak out when one opened up on them. Nonetheless, the war cry of the big 7.62 made several pause visibly. A couple more spilled over the fence and hit the grass running, unlimbering rifles as they came.

McKay's next burst knocked down two of the running figures. He swung the weapon left, began working methodically from east to west, laddering his bursts, firing three shots, then four, five, then three again, peeling climbers off the ornamental ironwork fence. Bullets were cracking over his head now, but he paid no attention. He was hitting the bastards hard, but they still kept coming . . .

From behind him came the hard, heavy *tuke* of a grenade launcher. A moment later a geyser of dense white smoke erupted near the southernmost point of the fence. Climbers began to drop off the fence like overripe fruit, and others running up behind fell back, batting at the smoke with their hands. Teargas.

McKay was on his feet, shouting "Take over!" at a startled Sam Sloan as he vaulted into the Sun Room and raced back toward the north side of the building. "Case, take her around onto East Exec and give enfilading fire across the South Lawn. Be ready to traverse and fire north too, because *here they come.*"

He burst out onto the promenade to see a ragged wave rolling across Pennsylvania Avenue.

He ripped off a burst from the hip. Though the range was long for a stunt like that—fifty meters or more—a couple of the gaunt, ragged runners went down. Well, he had a lot of targets.

He didn't race out to the end of the portico, but instead flopped down on his belly beside it, hoping to be able to pour flanking fire on anybody who managed to make it to the entryway. *Jeez, how many of these assholes are there?* There were forty or fifty rushing the perimeter, some brandishing clubs and chains, others holding rifles, shotguns, pistols. At the same time, unseen gunmen in the woods and brush churned out a volume of fire more savage even than the outburst that had greeted the flag's unfurling at dawn.

A dozen or so opted for the easy way, rushed in a body through the long-broken gates between the burned-out guardposts. Scarcely bothering to sight, he poured in a long burst. He saw one bandannaed head suddenly fly apart as his copper-jacketed slugs found the range. Then he chopped his bullet stream into them like a chainsaw. Bodies went everywhere.

The MG jammed.

One instant the gun was singing its head-busting song in his ears; the next moment silence hit him like a hammer. For a splinter of a second he froze, squeezing the trigger so hard he should have etched his fingerprints into the steel. But not for long. Billy McKay hadn't lived this long by choking when things got tight and hot.

He heard the slow hammer of Mobile One's .50

caliber from over his right shoulder, a metallic clangor like somebody whaling shit out of an oil drum with a ballpeen hammer. He hooked up the feed-tray cover of the M-60, and found that the belt was twisted. Mentally he cursed himself for being such a smart guy. He had fifty-round Australian ammo pouches—half-moon shaped, plastic, designed to clip onto the weapon's receiver—which kept the ammo belts from tangling and did away with the need for an assistant gunner. But he had to be clever, carry a couple of full, unboxed belts with him; *he* was going to be ready for anything that came along, and anyway those cartridge belts looked so stud crossed over his manly chest.

Under normal circumstances he had the eye and the instincts to get along without an A-gunner, firing only short bursts, knowing almost by feel when he needed a quick flip of the hand to smooth the belt's passage into the voracious MG. But he'd done all that dancing around, back and forth through the top-floor living quarters and storage rooms, trying to hold down both sides of the fort at once. So, naturally, the belt had got twisted up at the worst imaginable moment.

Though they'd faltered at first under his withering fire, the ragged crowd of attackers charged with new confidence the moment it stopped. Even at a time like this, McKay was taking it all in, marking the differences between this crew and the mob that had attacked before their breakout last year: that had been a panicky horde of bureaucrats in suits and ragged ghetto youth, driven beyond reason by the awful fact of the War. Sporadically armed with weapons looted from police—or pulled from secret caches by terrorist cadre eager to help things along—they had come on with ferocity and amazing bravery in the face of the devastating fire of the Guardians and the Secret Service contingent, but with little skill. Only their numbers, at least a thousand, had made them a menace to the tough, well-armed professionals playing Alamo inside.

This movie had a different cast entirely. The attackers were all white and male, lean as coyotes, with nary a suit among them. At least half of them had guns. And while sometimes they forgot themselves, jamming into a knot in the gateway to be chopped into stir-fry by McKay's M-60, most of them had the sense to spread out and run bent over, zigzagging to foul their enemy's aim.

"Casey," McKay barked. "What's your situation?"

"Least a dozen bad guys are on the lawn, skirmishing forward. They're using the bushes and Sam's CS for cover."

McKay tore the crimped belt from the receiver, ripped off the first half-dozen rounds from the damaged belt, threw them away, slapped the fresh end into the weapon, and slammed the feed-tray cover down. There was no more time to pull Mobile One back to where its powerful armament could cover the North Lawn, even if they dared; the North Lawn was much narrower than the South, and the attackers were across it already.

McKay hosed the crescent drive in front of the portico even as the assault wave reached it, knowing he was risking another hang-up but forced to take the risk. Several attackers fell howling to the pavement. The rest just rolled on.

"Mr. President—"

At Srinarampa's warning, MacGregor had moved up into the bedroom overlooking the entryway, beneath the portico's roof. He took with him a couple of clackers— electronic hand detonators for the Claymores Rogers had placed at the north and south entryways to the building.

Deafening silence ensued as attackers streamed onto

the porch. McKay's heart skidded to a stop. His worst-case scenario was coming true: he and his teammates tied up in a hot action with the enemy, unable to break off and without time to reach the President in time even if they could. *If Jeff freaks out now, we're going to be short one President.*

A sharp explosion shook the roof beneath McKay as though a giant fist had just slammed into the portico. McKay was halfway up, rising so that he could bend forward and get at least some fire into the entryway. What he saw was eerie, like something from a movie: a half-dozen armed men just vanished in a spray of blood and disjointed parts as hundreds of steel ballbearings riding the shockwave whiffed the length of the portico and out across the drive, striking marble columns and bouncing in all directions with a high keening sound. McKay felt a tug at his trouser leg as one whipped through his pants and into his shin.

He watched attackers flung away from the entry, spinning, falling as in slow motion, trailing streamers of blood. A good twenty were caught by the giant shotgunlike blast, most of them killed outright, the rest unlikely to survive without better medical care than they were likely to come by here in the ruins.

The survivors turned and ran. Stretching himself back out on his belly, McKay fired measured bursts to keep them headed the right way. He didn't fire over their heads. *The more I take care of now,* he thought as a spray of 7.62 bullets knocked dust from the back of a denim vest and pitched its occupant onto his face in the knee-high grass, *the fewer we'll have to deal with later.*

Even as those who could scrambled frantically over the fence or dashed out through the gate, McKay heard Sam's voice in his ear. "They're pulling back to the Ellipse, Billy."

For half an hour everybody held in place, waiting for a fresh assault. None came. Several wounded attackers still groaned piteously out by the entryway.

"For God's sake, Billy," MacGregor said through his communicator. "You just can't let them keep suffering like this."

McKay would have let his own buddies—or himself—bleed to death, if that's what it took to keep the President secure. But given the time that had passed without another attack, or even resumption of the firing, he relented. "Casey, pull around in front of the building. Tom, go ahead and take care of the wounded."

When Jeffrey MacGregor saw how Tom Rogers was helping the enemy wounded, he turned away with a retching sound. He was a compassionate man, and for most of the time since the One-Day War he'd lived a cloistered life beneath the Iowa landscape in Heartland. The horrors and adventures he'd experienced since then hadn't exactly inured him, but he now realized that some things couldn't be helped. Guardians medic Rogers was systematically slitting the throat of every fallen enemy who showed signs of life. Given that they had no manpower to take care of prisoners, given that without greater medical intervention than they had at their disposal few of the wounded would survive anyway, MacGregor knew it was the best thing; but he damned well didn't have to watch it.

Tom Rogers returned to Mobile One down in the sunken driveway, while Casey Wilson came up to take over from Sam Sloan, toting his long sniper's rifle. Sam went down to go back to work taking inventory.

As he did they held a council of war via their communicators, lying in place waiting for a fresh assault. McKay wanted to send Mobile One on the rampage through Lafayette Park, trying to clean out their opposition once and for all. Tom Rogers scotched the notion with a few quiet words.

"Too much risk, Billy. They might have some kind of antitank capability, and we can't afford to lose either man or machine." The fact that Rogers, his usual turret gunner, would probably have been one of the ones at risk didn't enter the former Green Beret's calculations. Of all the men—heroes and cowards and the vast array of plain old grunts just trying to get by with an unpunctured skin—McKay had known, Tom Rogers was the one man he truly believed didn't know the meaning of fear.

"If they'd had, like, rockets, wouldn't they have used them already?" Casey Wilson wanted to know.

"Not if they wanted to loot the place," Sam Sloan said. "They wouldn't want to blow up anything salvageable."

That raised again the question of just why there was *so much* that was salvageable still lying around, but this wasn't the time to debate that. "Is that what they wanted?" Casey Wilson asked, perplexed.

"Who knows?"

"You're right, Tom," McKay said. "We'll forget playing Rat Patrol for now. What I want to know right now is, just what the hell made them hit us so hard? If they tried probing attacks they could have got us to burn up a lot of ammo without taking too many casualties."

"I don't know that, either," Sloan said. "What I do know is that I was shocked at the way they came on in the face of our grenade launchers and that fifty-cal. I know *I* wouldn't have liked running right into those guns."

"Maybe we can parley," Tom Rogers suggested.

McKay grimaced. "That may be our only choice —that or a breakout, if things get too hairy. Right now, what I guess we're gonna do is just hunker down and keep watch.''

Sam continued taking stock of the treasures that lay miraculously untouched inside the battered building, aided by Dr. S. Occasionally a shot cracked in. Twice McKay heard the knock of Casey's noise-suppressed rifle, knew the former fighter jock had picked off some unfortunate unwary enough to expose a few square centimeters of himself to Casey's searching eye. Other than that, lots and lots of nothing happened.

The sun fell down into the haze lying along the Potomac. Sam Sloan broke out a couple of flare pistols from the stores that had been left behind and had the obliging Indian doctor run them up to Casey and McKay on the roof. They broke out ration packs and ate in position. McKay was beginning to feel as if his bones were turning to lead, but there was no time to rest—least of all with darkness on its way. The Guardians had no place to hide; night was all on their enemies' side.

Then as the last feeble color of daylight was beginning to fade, Sam Sloan said, "You'd better come down here, McKay. We've got company."

CHAPTER
THREE ─────────────────────

Taking advantage of the sunny, sweltering July day, Yevgeny Maximov, owner and proprietor of the Federated States of Europe, sat at his ease in a deck chair on the ramparts of his headquarters. The ancient bulk of Schloss Ehrenbreitstein squatted atop a sheer cliff overlooking the confluence of the Rhine and Neckar rivers, giving a superb view up and down the green Rhine Valley and over the city of Koblenz, which had been little damaged by the War. Far away to the north, the sun glanced off the white hull of a Köln-Düsseldorf hydrofoil ferry skimming south. Returning the hydrofoils to service was a special pride of the FSE, though with the state of emergency on, only those with pressing official business were permitted to ride them. Mostly they ran empty these days, but they still ran regularly: appearances must be kept up.

Maximov wore khaki shorts and polarized sunglasses, and a winged silver reflecting contrivance slung under his chin to even his tan. In spite of these appurtenances, he resembled nothing so much as a caricature of Neanderthal Man. His head was huge, with a granite bluff of brow, a mostly shapeless nose, small keen eyes, full lips fringed by a heavy but immaculately barbered beard. His huge shoulders were as heavy as a bear's. A sizable paunch bulged out over the front of the shorts, covered with grizzled dark fur, but it was clear at a glance that there was nothing soft about this man.

He sipped at his drink, glanced about at the splendid view—encompassing the river, the throbbing city, the forested hills, and several of his "assistants" arranged in fetching attitudes around the terrace—and sighed in contentment.

Despite the bluster of warm wind along the cliff top, he heard the precise click of heels on flagstones behind him, and realized he'd expressed his contentment prematurely. "Yes, Nathalie, *ma petite*. What have you come to plague me with now?"

His aide-de-camp stopped with a final double click and stood erect beside his chair. "I have word from our forces in North America," she said, "and I am *not* your *petite*."

The massive head swiveled a few degrees, a grandly thatched eyebrow rose. He was the most powerful man in Europe—probably the most powerful man alive. Was it conceivable that he, Chairman Maximov, could be addressed in such an impertinent manner?

But of course. He could command yes-men—and yes-women—by the batallion, by the army. For his factotum he required someone who had a mind and wasn't afraid to use it. Or to speak it.

"And what have our conquering heroes to report?" he inquired.

"They've got a team in downtown Baltimore. They

confirm the burning wreckage our watchers observed to be that of an F-15 fighter jet dispatched to intercept a cargo plane that refused to identify itself.''

A ponderous nod. "And the intruder?"

"They haven't found its wreckage yet, sir."

Maximov snorted. "Do they believe it was the Guardians and their little President, then?"

"Colonel Leveque believes so. He reports he's already made arrangements for dividing the reward."

"Hah!" A hairy slab of hand slammed down on the cedar arm of the deck chair, causing it to flex dangerously. "The fools. They've let the damned Guardians slip through their fingers again, and twice fools for not even realizing it!"

He raised a finger. One of his assistants swayed forward, bearing a telephone—antique, white, with golden trim—on a silver tray. It was in his mind to order some summary executions. . . . He checked himself. From his earliest days, starving and penniless on the docks of Hamburg, when he kept himself warm through frigid Elbe nights by assuring himself that one day he'd rule, if not the world, then a substantial chunk of it, he had told himself over and over that he was never going to play the cartoon tyrant. He would use power, not the other way around; ordering executions now would be sheer petulance. *And if I started making an end to every operative who let the Guardians outwit him,* he thought wryly, *soon I'd have no agents left at all.*

The assistant halted at his right arm. For a moment he simply sat and enjoyed filling his hairy nostrils with the musk of sun-heated female skin. "Never mind," he said, raising his hand dismissively. He noticed a few flecks of dead grass, summer dry and windblown, caught in the chestnut tangle of the assistant's pubic hair. With a couple of matter-of-fact swipes he swept the fragments away. The girl stood still, gave him a smile with some of the day's warmth in it. "Take that thing away; I've no need of it after all. You and you, bring a chair for Ms. Frechette, and some hot tea for her."

Nathalie Frechette lowered herself into another deck chair placed at Maximov's left by two more nude and nubile assistants with a pointed sniff. Since her arrival at the castle several weeks ago, she had been at pains on several occasions to point out her disapproval of Maximov's "assistants." At the moment he didn't feel like rising to her bait. Instead, he crossed his hands over his paunch like a circus bear that had just finished a pizza, regarding her under heavy lids.

She was a solid woman in her mid-thirties, of medium height, with a round face and straight nose and short, almost painfully straight dark-orange hair. She wore a dark-green blouse, a jacket and skirt of a peculiar green tweed. *She might be an attractive girl,* Maximov mused, *if she didn't work so hard to make herself drab.*

After a while she began to fidget under his placid ursine scrutiny. "Very well," she said, shifting her tweed-clad rump in the deck chair, "if it is indeed true that the Guardians have once more eluded our forces—which I myself doubt—what are your orders?"

"First, learn wisdom, child. I have been dealing with these troublesome Guardians for over a year, and one thing I have come to take for granted concerning them: if we do not have bodies—positively identified ones— we do not have the Guardians."

"But, really, Chairman! A fighter jet aircraft against an unarmed transport plane?" She shook her head.

"A jet fighter airplane that was destroyed," Maximov reminded her gently. "How that may have come about I have no idea; I am no expert in aerial combat. One of the Guardians, as it happens, is. We have a ruined fighter and no sign at all of this other aircraft. Given the Guardians' past performance, one draws certain inferences.''

She shook her head as if trying to clear water from her ears. Clearly she was vexed, but equally clearly she was unwilling to push the issue further.

An assistant, white-blond and willowy, approached and set down a silver teapot and matching sugar bowl and a fine china cup on a wheeled tray beside her. She smiled, mockingly, withdrew silently, unfazed by Frechette's answering glare.

"If you truly believe the Guardians and President MacGregor have escaped, there's only one place they would have gone," Frechette said, ladling several spoonfuls of sugar into her tea. That was her one vice, Maximov recalled. He nodded as she continued, "Washington, D.C. Therefore, I'd suggest ordering Colonel Leveque to mobilize as many troops as possible and move them into the capital immediately. He can cordon off the city, send troops in to root out the gangsters.''

"Ridiculous." Her head jerked back as if he'd slapped her. "Forgive me, child, I spoke too harshly. Able as you are, you're young, and don't know everything yet. If our Colonel Leveque mobilized every man he could spare and every man he couldn't, he still could not cordon off the city in a way that would make it impossible for the Guardians to slip out again with MacGregor. These are experts we are dealing with, men at the absolute peak of their craft by virtue both of background and of training. That is why I found it necessary to assemble a similar team to send against them.

"As to digging them out—you know as well as I that the Expeditionary Force hasn't got twenty thousand men in North America, and almost every one of them is needed where he is so that we can hold what we've got. Sending a combat team into the gang-infested rubble of Washington would mean tying at least a thousand men up for the good God alone knows how long. And we're already bogged down in too many urban sinkholes —Chicago, Kansas City, Houston, to name but a few. No, we need something smaller scale. More discreet."

He took another sip from his drink as he considered the problem. It was a sixteen-ounce glass two-thirds encased in what looked like a thick Styrofoam sleeve. The sleeve was in fact a solar-powered miniature cooling unit, which kept the Chairman's drink chilled to a precise degree. It was a high-tech toy sent as tribute by Trajan, his viceroy for North America, now defunct. It was vodka, neat, of course; for all Maximov's fluency in French—or German, or English, or Italian—and for all the Continental elegance of his surroundings and dress, he was still a Ukrainian by birth.

He unsnapped the strap of the Mylar reflector from behind his neck, cast it aside, and stood. He stretched, sighed, scratched his belly, and moved forward on his thick legs to peer over the weathered stone rampart. The Rhine slouched olive drab beneath him. The heat of reflected sunlight beat up against his face even this high. He could spit from here and hit the river, and it was all his, from the Alps to the North Sea; splendid, splendid. He gestured for Frechette to join him. Hesitantly, she stepped forward, not looking over the edge. She feared heights.

"Chairman Maximov, I understand the sacrifices you make—for all of us. But I still can't understand why you surround yourself with—with—" She looked from side to side till her gaze lit on a beautiful Eurasian woman, tiny and perfect as a porcelain figure, sitting with her moon-pale buttocks perched on the weathered stone of the parapet, brushing out lustrous midnight hair so long its ends touched the pavement when she walked. "Them. It's—it's degrading to women."

"Nathalie, my dear child, I will tell you a thing. I began with nothing, a penniless refugee, seeking work during worldwide Depression when no work was to be had, not even by the native sons of the countries whose guest I was. I learned the value of saving, of deferring gratification of present wants for future benefit. I have made sacrifices in my life, sacrificed everything I had except life itself more times than I have toes and fingers. But do you know what? As a starveling boy I promised myself that I would make no sacrifice that was not *necessary*, never stint myself when I had means sufficient to my ends in hand. And throughout my life I have kept the pact I made with that boy. And do you know? It made the lean times easier to endure."

He turned toward her. "The simple fact is that I like to look at naked women. Therefore, I arrange to do so whenever I so desire, such as now. Shameful, perhaps. But I am only human."

She was studying the square toes of her severe black shoes. Naive as she was, she really believed that Maximov, up here in his castle surrounded by his toothsome assistants, suffered more than the most wretched refugees starving in the rubble of Amsterdam, on account of having taken the burden of the destiny of all mankind upon his massive shoulders.

He wasn't going to get any misty-eyed looks of admiration from her this time; the presence of his assistants made her too uncomfortable for that. But while his words didn't make her discomfiture and her feminist outrage go away, they did make her feel unworthy for feeling them.

She started to raise her head, froze. From the look of distracted concentration on her face Maximov deduced she was getting a message over her personal communicator, through the tiny bone-conduction speaker taped behind her ear—a device quite similar to those used by his adversaries, the Guardians, and in fact looted from America. He himself refused to wear any such thing. Was he some kind of lackey, to be constantly on call?

"They've located the Hercules," she said, raising her head with a glint of triumph in her cow-brown eyes. "They've spotted the wreckage near the ruins of a cement plant north of Washington, D.C."

He shrugged. "Perhaps I was wrong. For once I should be pleased to be so."

"They've already got a chopper on the scene—we're getting live reports, relayed via satellite. Would you like a receiver brought to you?"

He held up his hand and shook his head. This was not a soccer match, and he required no play-by-play account. Instead he lumbered over to the deck chair, sat down, and picked up his glass again, which had of course been refilled.

Frechette drifted behind as if in a trance. "Wait a minute—the description of the wreckage—the craft appears to have made a successful crash landing."

Maximov cocked an eyebrow at her.

She reported that a party was making its way into the wreckage. They sat in silence broken only by the wind. Then she relayed what they'd learned: three dead, two bodies identifiable as being neither Guardians nor Jeffrey MacGregor, the third battered beyond recognition but not appearing to match any of the fugitives in body type.

Maximov nodded. "Cargo?"

Her lips showed the ghost of movement as she spoke
for the benefit of the microphone taped to her larynx.
Then: "None. The aircraft is empty."

"You may tell Colonel Leveque that he need trouble
himself no longer over the problem of how to dispense
the reward. It's clear he's let his prey slip through his
fingers."

His factotum wouldn't meet his eyes. He laughed, a
deeply resonant sound, gusty as the wind itself. "Well,
then. I know how to handle this. I think your pred-
ecessor could use a vacation from tutoring our brave but
boneheaded General Maitland in the subtleties of political administration.

"Get me California. Ivan Vesensky is going to Washington."

CHAPTER
FOUR ─────────────────────────────

Billy McKay was dying to find out just who the hell this company Sam Sloan was talking about were, but he waited until Tom Rogers de-assed Mobile One and turned up on the roof before he went below, entrusting his pet Maremont to the former Green Beret. It didn't matter whether Sloan's mystery guest was Elvis, Jesus, or E.T. They just couldn't afford to do without having all of their observation posts manned by somebody with keen eyesight and the ability and readiness to shoot, even for a moment.

But neither singers, saviors, nor extraterrestrials awaited Billy McKay. Instead an incredibly skinny Puerto Rican kid who looked as if he might weigh 120 pounds soaking wet stood in the foyer. He was wearing cammie pants with many pockets, tennis shoes that seemed to consist of holes and Velcro straps, and a curiously bulky army jacket (which, despite the heat,

was buttoned almost to the neck over a black T-shirt).
He was unarmed, at least as far as McKay could see.
Sam Sloan stood to one side, not quite covering him
with his Galil.

"Hey man, what's happenin'?" the kid inquired with
a cheerful nod toward McKay.

"Who the fuck is this?"

"I'm Sammy," the newcomer offered.

"Beats the heck out of me," Sloan said. "I was
rooting around downstairs when suddenly I heard a
noise behind me. I turned around and there he was."
Sloan's eyes skidded away from McKay's. McKay
seldom passed up an opportunity to ride him for his
black-shoe, surface Navy background, so manifestly
unsuited to the grunt combat environment in which the
Guardians operated. He'd let himself get snuck up on
by a ghetto kid in K-Mart cammies, and he expected to
take grief for it.

But for once giving Sam Sloan crap was the furthest
thing from McKay's mind. "Okay, Sammy. How the
hell did you get in here and what do you want?"

Even though the former marine was big enough to
just pick him up and bite his head off like a sideshow
geek, Sammy was elaborately unimpressed. He grinned,
showing yellow tilted teeth. "Hey, man, take it easy. I
know how to get in and out of here; we all do." Before
the thunderstruck Guardians could press him for
details, he dropped another HE round right onto the
Great Seal at their feet. "You guys got the President,
don't you?"

For once in his life Billy McKay was struck stone
speechless. "What, ah, makes you think that, son?"
Sam managed after a moment.

"You the Guardians, ain't you?"

McKay and Sloan traded looks. Since keeping their presence in the President's entourage secret from the news teams would have been impossible, Major Crenna —the mystery man who had created the Guardians and ramrodded Project Blueprint—had gone the other way with a big media campaign about the President's elite new "bodyguards." They had even had their pictures in *Parade* magazine, for Chrissake. It had borne dividends in what had turned out to be the Guardians' real mission, assembling the Blueprint for Renewal in the wake of World War III; folks were just naturally more inclined to help people whose pictures they had seen in the paper. But at times like this it made security a royal pain in the ass.

"You're Billy McKay," the kid said to McKay. He turned to Sloan with a thoughtful frown. "And you must be, uh, Rogers. That Army dude."

Sloan slapped on his best down-home country grin. "Nope. I'm much prettier than he is."

"Oh, so you're Casey Wilson. The fighter pilot. Shit, man, I been wantin' to meet you for years."

Sloan's grin joined the powdered plaster and ancient leaves dusted across the floor. McKay cleared his throat. "Just who the hell wants to know if we got the President or not? And why?" He let his hand drop to the butt of his .45, nestled in a Milt Sparks custom fast-draw rig for serious conversation.

"I'm from Soong. And he wants to talk to the President right away."

"If you don't tighten the set-screws on your jaw, McKay," Sam Sloan remarked after a minute, "you're going to get your shoelaces caught in your lower teeth."

"Well, of all the—" McKay ran out of steam and stopped. There he was, a former Parris Island drill in-

structor, and he wasn't even able to summon up the pro-
fanity to suit the occasion. It was a hell of a thing.

"What was that name again, Billy?" Tom Rogers's
voice asked softly in his ear. McKay had dialed his
microphone to maximum gain before coming into the
meeting so that the other two and MacGregor could
listen in. He repeated the question aloud.

"Soong," the kid repeated politely. "The Lord of the
Tidal Basin."

"I recollect it now," Rogers said. "The backup
White House Detail was headed by a fella by that name.
Ethnic Chinese from Thailand. Ex-Special Forces.
Good man." A pause, then, "I don't know about the
rest of that, though."

"Well, kid," McKay said, "Thank this Soong of
yours for the invitation. But we're a little too busy to go
creepy-crawling around through the rubble this time of
night. There's a little matter of a couple hundred bad
guys who got us penned in here and want to shoot at
us."

Sammy sneered, "The Red Dog Family. They won't
bother you no more tonight."

"Yeah? And just how the hell you figure that?"

"Cause Soong put the word on them, man. And he's
the maximum man on this side of town." He shook his
head as if wondering whether McKay was smart enough
to change his own underwear unassisted. "Why you
think this place ain't all trashed out, anyway, man?
Look around. Hell, anybody these days sell his mother
to the Arabs for just the chance to grab a handful or two
of what's in the cupboards here. Why you think nobody
do that?"

"He's got a point," Casey observed.

"Soong tells them this place off limits. Anybody

comes in here, anybody fucks with anything, he dies bad, man, real bad.''

"So why the hell were these Red Dog assholes in such a hurry to get in here earlier?'' McKay asked.

"Shit, man, you too full of questions. They thought maybe you trespassers, if they rousted you out of here Soong would let 'em fill up some shopping carts, like as a reward, man. They wanted to get to you before we did. Only we finally sent word for them to lay off.'' He shifted his weight, the rubber soles of his sneakers crunching fine debris underfoot. "So, go get the President and let's get out of here.''

McKay scratched the back of his bull neck. "Sam? Tom? Casey? What the fuck, over?''

"Looks as if we'd better talk to our friend Soong,'' Sam said. The other two concurred.

McKay fumbled at his pockets, remembered he'd smoked his last cigar that morning. "Shit,'' he said. "Okay. Sloan, looks like you and me are gonna take a little walk. I hate to leave this place short two, but from what the kid says, maybe it'll be okay.''

"We may not have much chance, Billy,'' Rogers said. "We need to make contact.''

"What about the President?'' Sammy persisted.

McKay shook his head. "Uh-uh. No way.''

"Listen, man, I was told to bring the President back. He's comin' or nobody.''

"Now, listen here, shorty,'' McKay growled. "You go back and tell this Soong—belay that. You're gonna take us to this big dude of yours, we're gonna tell him in person just what he can do with trying to shove the President of the United States around.''

"I'm not takin' you nowhere without the President!'' the kid shouted, olive features darkening.

"The fuck you aren't!"

"The fuck I am!" He tore open the front of his Army jacket, sending buttons every which way, pulled up the front of his black Motley Crue T-shirt. McKay found himself staring at the words FRONT TOWARD ENEMY pressed into a smooth, slightly convex olive-drab surface.

"Well fuck me to tears," he said, "little bastard's got a Claymore strapped to his chest."

Sammy brandished a clacker in his skinny hand. "I'm ready to use it too, man. You don't push me around."

"Now, now," Sloan said smoothly, slowly releasing his assault rifle to hang from the Israeli-style sling around his neck. "Let's not get carried away here."

"If it's important," MacGregor said, entering the discussion for the first time, "I can go along with him."

"Negative," McKay said, respectfully but emphatically. He didn't say *sir,* and he tried to keep his eyes from rolling upward toward the room where the President was still forted up. He wasn't going to give away any more information than necessary.

"You've got to understand, son," Sloan said, "that even if we do have the President here, we can't very well just let him wander off into the darkness on your say-so. Now, the rest of your . . . friends . . . have been preserving the White House just as it was for the President to return, am I right?"

The boy nodded.

"Well, if you think about it, then once the President got back here it might not be right for him to go running off again, as well as not smart. Can you see that?"

He had the kid nodding right along. It was one of his special talents; he could get a PLO hit man to make a contribution to B'nai B'rith if he had a few minutes to work on him. "So, why don't you just lead Lieutenant McKay and myself to where this Mr. Soong is waiting, and we'll explain the situation to him. I'm sure he'll understand."

The kid went a few shades paler. "Oh shit, I can't do that. They said I had to bring the President."

Forestalling an outburst from McKay with a slight urgent hand signal, Sloan said, "But we've already explained that's impossible, son. Let us talk to your people; it'll be okay."

"But Andy! Shit, he'll—he'll—" The kid broke off, looking nervously all around as if expecting Andy to come erupting right out of the walls like something in a horror movie. *Nightmare on Pennsylvania Avenue.*

McKay was impressed. Here was a kid who was willing to walk around with a fucking *Claymore* strapped to his chest, and the mere thought of this Andy turned his shit right straight to water.

"Kid," he growled, "whoever this Andy is, I promise I eat punks like him for breakfast. I'm the leader of the Guardians, not a pack of Girl Scouts."

Sam Sloan shut his eyes very, very tightly. But the kid just laughed. "Well, hey, man, that's fine." He tried manfully to contain the tremor in the words. "I'll do it, you know? I'll take you with me, and you can say that to Andy. Shit, man, he'll forget all about being pissed at *me*."

The route led out through a window just this side of the steel barrier that cut off the main building from the West Wing, across once-manicured flower beds that had now disappeared underneath a dense tangle of weeds, along the flank of the President's executive offices, hugging the building around to West Executive Avenue.

There was little danger of their being observed, unless they shone flashlights everywhere and whistled "The Stars and Stripes Forever." Most of the trees and shrubs in this part of the grounds, some growing right up against the building, were still alive, having exploded into startling profusion in the rains.

McKay and Sloan looked at each other as they picked their way through the undergrowth. It was little short of a miracle that the enemies who surrounded them hadn't slipped across the street from the renovated Executive Office Building to make good use of precisely this route. Was it possible this Soong was what the kid claimed?

Half a moon hung aloof from a few nondescript clouds, silvering the derelict vehicles abandoned in the street. Sawhorse-type wooden traffic barriers had been set up at the top of the steps to the EOB, barring the entryway, whose glass had gone the way of the buffalo during the bombardment, like most of the glass in the city. Sammy peered up and down the street.

"C'mon. We shouldn't have no trouble if we're spotted, but better not take no chances." He slipped across.

After him went McKay, bent over, running with surprising silence for his bulk. He carried one of their special-lot .45 MP-5 submachine guns with integral silencer. If they ran into trouble on the way, he was in a position to take care of it without kicking up much fuss. If that weren't possible, Sam Sloan was covering from the other side of the street with his Galil-203, with a shotgun-style MP round up the spout and a whole vest full of grenades, and *he* could make as much noise as you wanted.

A moment, and Sloan joined the two by the barricade. McKay gave him a wolf's grin as he glanced down at one of the traffic barrels set at either end and recoiled as if he'd just been burned, barely choking back a cry. Pounded into the barrel's cement core was a length of steel reinforcement bar, and impaled on it was a human skull, ghost white in the moonlight, a few dark shrivels of dried meat sticking to it. There were several of the grisly mementos, one fresh enough to stink and buzz with flies.

"We tell people to keep out of here," Sammy remarked. "But there's always someone who don't get the message, you know?"

They slipped through the echoing emptiness of the EOB's corridors. They smelled of mildewed paper and acoustic tile and, faintly, death. McKay was surprised to find absent the aromas he remembered from derelict buildings in his Pittsburgh youth: piss, puke, cheap wine, rotting food, and rancid human grease. It was one of those little details that crept up and hit him from behind, every now and then, to remind him just how severe a catastrophe the human race had been through.

Sammy moved confidently, seeming to know how to step without dropping his foot on broken glass or less identifiable debris without even looking. Sloan and McKay picked their way after him rather more cautiously.

"If we run into trouble," Sam Sloan subvocalized from the rear, "I hope he has sense enough to let us handle it." He knew full well that the ferocious backlash of the mine strapped to the youth's chest would still have plenty of energy left to blast them both to bits after it vaporized him.

McKay shrugged. He'd already decided that if the shit hit the fan he'd just shoot the kid and not give him a chance to wipe them all out.

Sammy led them out a door flanked by the same

gruesome ornaments as the other, across Seventeenth, jogging briefly left, to head west two blocks along F Street between solid monolithic slabs of buildings. At Nineteenth they went south past Interior North and South to Constitution Avenue.

Ahead of them a line of trees and a chest-high wall of undergrowth screened the Reflecting Pool from view. "This way," Sammy whispered, moving left along the narrow paved drive.

"Enemy's that way," grunted McKay. Actually Sammy was heading them toward the grounds of the fallen Washington Monument, south of the Ellipse where the attacks had come from, but it didn't take much imagination to figure some of the bad guys might be hanging out south of Constitution.

Sammy shook his head. "No, no, it's okay. Trust me."

"I'm tempted to shoot the little fuck on general principles, just for saying that," McKay said under his breath. But they followed. Their guide led them almost back to Seventeenth Street before cutting south through the trees.

Once through, Sammy halted. McKay and Sloan stopped behind him, Sloan quivering with alertness, McKay apparently more relaxed, but coiled taut inside, ready to spring in any direction.

"The pool," Sloan said over the comm. "It's full of water."

McKay started to ask him what the fuck was the big deal about that. Then he remembered the fountains on the White House ground were empty except for a muddy sludgy residue at the bottom. The big cement pool was full of water, gently moving, an image of the half-moon breaking into infinite jigsaw designs on its surface.

"It's Sammy," their guide said softly to the surrounding dark. "I brought 'em."

From the brush to their left came a piercing whistle. Sloan jumped. McKay twitched the thick shrouded barrel of his MP in that direction. "It's cool," said Sammy, showing teeth in amusement. "Follow me. We got a reception planned."

McKay started forward. Sloan hung back. "What does he mean? What if it's a trap?"

"Then Tom and Case come down here in Mobile One and shoot many, many assholes, and then they drive the President the hell out of here and start all over somewhere else," McKay replied. "Move your butt, Navy boy. Wanna live forever?"

"It's not such a bad idea." He spoke to the broad darkness of McKay's retreating back.

As they came to the foot of the Reflecting Pool flame blossomed to either side of them. McKay came within a hair's breadth of cutting loose with his submachine gun, then realizing it was torches, rags soaked in gasoline and wrapped around the ends of sticks touched off with lighters, not muzzle flashes. Sloan let out a hissing breath through clenched teeth.

Sammy walked backward before them, still grinning. They followed. More torches flared alight, pacing pair by pair, every twenty meters along the entire six-hundred-meter length of the pool.

"Check these dudes out, Sloan," McKay said, sub-vocalizing so that only the microphone picked it up. "Ever seen anything like 'em?"

"Yes. Road gypsies."

They stood in silent ranks between the torches: whites, Hispanics, Orientals, bare chests turned rosy amber by the yellow glow, here and there a black looking like a statue carved from hand-rubbed ebony. They were decked out in extravagant style: paint on face and body, headbands, ornaments of feathers and cloth and beads. They were well armed, with weapons ranging from mini-Uzis in shoulder holsters through Belgian FNs as long as crutches, to a Soviet RPG-7V antitank rocket launcher tucked negligently under a bare arm. One dude even had the double tanks of an ancient flamethrower strapped on his back and the nozzle in his hands.

"Shee-it," McKay said. "Looks like whoever put this together saw *Apocalypse Now* more times than was good for him."

"Welcome to the heart of darkness," Sloan said. "Are you sure they're on *our* side?"

"Nope."

They reached the end of the pool, passed between more torch bearers as they crossed the drive that encircled the Lincoln Memorial. As they approached the steps leading up to the vast whiteness of the monument, unseen hands fired flare guns into gasoline-impregnated piles of flammable debris to either side. Huge bonfires flared up, smearing the front of the memorial with a hideous yellow-orange glow.

At the foot of the steps McKay and Sloan stopped. Silent outlandish warriors were packed tightly to either side of them. Sammy had vanished as if Scotty had beamed him up.

Way back in the memorial's gloom, firelight-brushed, the larger-than-life figure of old Abe Lincoln sitting in his chair of state was still intact. From the marble president's right-hand side appeared a single figure. It was an enormously squat man clad in a black robe that gave back blood-red silken highlights, his huge splayed feet in sandals, his face moon broad and moon round, topped with a dome of balding skull. The nose was a wide flat triangle, almost African, the eyes obsidian crescents.

"Welcome, Mr. President," he was saying as he stepped forward to the head of the stairs, his voice deep and sonorous as the tolling of a great bronze gong. "I am Soong. I—"

He broke off, the great smooth brow wrinkling as he stared in puzzlement at McKay and Sloan.

And from the darkness beyond the torchlight a voice screamed, "Get back, Chief! *We've fucking been betrayed!*"

CHAPTER
FIVE ─────────────────────

"Casey," Billy McKay subvocalized, "I think we got trouble."

He and Sloan never had a chance. For an instant he tensed, ready to spring to the top of the steps and try standing off the crowd with one burly arm locked around Soong's fat throat and the muzzle of his submachine gun crammed in his ear. He let the moment pass; it just didn't feel right, somehow.

Then Soong's men were all over them. Strong hands gripped them, twisted weapons from their grasps. Gun muzzles prodded their Kevlar-armored torsos. Through it all Soong stood unmoving at the head of the steps, legs braced wide, head bowed, gazing down upon them like Buddha perplexed.

"You need a hand, Billy?" he heard Casey Wilson say.

"Negative—not just yet, anyway. But stand by. And

if you come, be ready to hit 'em hard—there's hundreds of the bastards and some of them have antitank."

To their left the crowd parted as a man thrust angrily through. He was a short son of a bitch, no more than five-five, five-six, slim and trim, with a wrestler's shoulders and neck, almost disproportionately thick. The way he carried his head thrust forward made him resemble a big dog, a greyhound walking on its hind legs, and he had a long dog's face with a lantern jaw and heavy nose, black eyes glaring from beneath emphatic brows. His hair was black and curly, cut short to his skull, and he wasn't wearing war paint. He had on a light-hued military shirt with epaulettes, baggy trousers of the same color bloused into combat boots, and some kind of immense double-action horse pistol—McKay guessed it was a Redhawk .44 Magnum—riding in a shoulder holster beneath his right armpit.

"What the fuck is going on here?" he shrieked, spittle flying from his lips. "Where's the President?"

He thrust himself right up in front of the two captives. "You haven't got the President, huh?" he yelled, not waiting for an answer. "You're trying to bluff your way in here. Is that it? Is that it? Answer me! Where's that little fucker Sammy? I'll pull out his asshole and wrap his intestines around his neck."

He glowered up at McKay as if preparing to bite him. "Thought you could put something over on us, big guy?" He pushed McKay hard—more of an open-handed punch against the breastbone.

About four half-naked dudes in feathers went sailing over McKay's shoulders as he jack-knifed forward, tearing his arms loose to grab the little puke and twist off some of his favorite parts. The man danced back as others lunged forward to seize McKay's arms. A look of sheer hatred twisted his face until it seemed the skin would split wide open and he reached for the outsized grips of his .44.

Then his face relaxed, his hand dropped away from the pistol butt, and he laughed. "Very good, very good. You have spirit, hah. I like that." For the first time McKay realized he spoke with some kind of accent he couldn't place.

Soong gazed down from the head of the steps, blinking slowly. "Perhaps we should hear what they have to say, Andy," he said, his voice surprisingly mild.

The smaller man nodded tautly, tipping his head forward and gazing up under his eyebrows at McKay and Sloan. McKay still had men hanging off him like Christmas-tree ornaments. He growled low in his throat. Sloan shot him a warning glance; he shut up.

"We're the Guardians," Sloan said.

"I know that," said Soong.

Sloan licked his lips, nodded. He glanced at the men at the left and the right of him. "Excuse me," he said, quietly confident, and took a step forward. His arms slid out of his captors' grasp as if they were greased. Sloan was the sort of guy who could pull a move like that off. He was still under the gun, though, and acted accordingly. "I won't try to dissemble, Mr. Soong. We have the President. As you may know, we've been on the run since we broke him out of Heartland a month ago. We just barely managed to get him into Washington, D.C., and have been under attack ever since we reached the White House. So I think you can understand it if we're a little, ah, cautious.

"Also—in all due respect—I have to ask you: Do you really think it's appropriate for the President of the United States to come when you call him?"

Andy's eyebrows had worked their way closer

together like horny caterpillars as he listened. "He's talking shit, Captain. It's an insult—"

Soong held up a hand. "No, no. He is correct. It would not befit the President's dignity to come running to my summons. Foolish of me not to think of it, very foolish."

Andy's manner underwent a sudden change at Soong's words. "You're kidding us, Captain," he said, holding his head low like a dog that expects to be kicked. "You tested them, to see if they were brave and strong, to see if this MacGregor has the dignity to be President. Now we know. You are our wise Captain."

Soong clucked. "Oh, Andy." But his bland smile was a little wider as he looked at the captives again.

"I am certain that President MacGregor would be honored to receive you and your lieutenants in the White House," Sam Sloan said. "Tomorrow—after he's had a decent night's sleep. It's been a hell of a few weeks."

Soong smiled openly, signaling appreciative laughter all around. "Are you nuts?" McKay said without moving his lips. The words went clearly to Sloan over the communicator.

"Are you?" Sloan shot back the same way. "We need allies. Here they are. You ever heard about looking a gift horse in the mouth, city boy?"

"Billy, this is President MacGregor. I think Sam's right. And I'm willing to meet with this Soong and his people. Looks like our only choice."

McKay shrugged. "Roger that, Mr. President. It's your play, Sloan."

"Let them go," Soong said. He didn't raise his voice, but the words carried clearly above the murmur of the mob at the Guardians' backs.

Sloan's watchdogs stepped back. An instant later

McKay's did, too, with a certain visible reluctance. In a moment the bizarre warriors had once again formed ranks to either side of the two Guardians, leaving them in a shifting pool of torchlight puddled at the base of the marble steps.

"These people are hard-core crazy," McKay sub-vocalized to Sloan.

"My friends," Soong said, raising his arms. "It is as we hoped. Our President has returned to resume his rightful place at the seat of this nation's government. Tomorrow we shall welcome him back to the White House."

A cheer billowed up from the darkness around and the double line of torches stretching back to the foot of the Reflecting Pool. Amid the tumult Soong descended to the base of the steps, laid his hands on the Guardians' shoulders. "It seems we have waited years for your return, my friends. But we have kept the faith. Now we are rewarded."

"Our country will thank you and your people for what you have done, Mr. Soong," Sloan said. "I can assure you that you have President MacGregor's gratitude as well."

This was getting too deep for Billy McKay to wade through. "I don't want to spoil the party," he growled, "but while we're standing here the President's still holed up in the White House by half the unattached assholes in North America."

Sloan winced.

"The Red Dog Family isn't so bad," Soong said. "We gave them our permission to camp by the White House, as long as they left it and its grounds alone."

"They broke their word," Andy thrust in. "Need a good lesson, hah?"

Somehow he had come in to stand between the Guardians and Soong. "You boys go back now, the way you came. We come to you tomorrow to see the President, ten hundred hours."

"What about them Red Dogs?" McKay asked stubbornly.

The smaller man's eyes flashed. "You don't worry about nothing," he said in a voice that indicated clearly that McKay was on his list. "We take care of them."

"But, can we trust them, man?" Casey Wilson asked.

Billy McKay was back on the roof behind his trusty M-60, feeling as if somebody had sandpapered his eyeballs. He couldn't remember ever having been so tired, not in SOG-SWAC, not in Force RECON, not in the peacekeeping force in the Root in '82. At least he had his hands on some decent hardware again. His little Heckler and Koch submachine gun had seemed awfully puny in the midst of that crazy bunch by the memorial. He stretched, fought down a yawn. Three hours since they'd slipped back into the White House, three more grinding endless hours of pushing his eyeballs into the night. He wasn't sure how much longer he could take.

"Soong led A-teams for SF in Southeast Asia," Tom Rogers said. "He's a good man."

"Well, he sure got a collection of escaped doorknobs like I never laid eyes on before," McKay said. "And there's somebody moving around out there. I think those Red Dog mothers are getting cranked up to make another try at us."

He'd no sooner spoken than he heard a heavy, dull *crump!* from somewhere. There was a whistling, then a sudden sear of white light among the bedraggled trees of Lafayette Park. A moment later a hot shockwave hit him in the face, an explosion bulged in his eardrums. By that time he already had his face buried in his forearms.

A moment later he heard another crash from behind him. Two Guardians and President MacGregor were babbling in his ears. Across their commotion came the sounds of screams from the park.

"What's going *on?*" Sam finally got through from his position on the south deck of the promenade.

Before McKay could answer, the heavy distant sound came again, like a giant drum struck once. It was echoed a heartbeat later by a smaller noise, higher pitched. "Mortars," McKay said, then ducked his head again as the rounds landed north and south of the embattled White House. "Sounds like an eighty-one-millimeter your way. Up front here they got themselves a four-deuce no less."

"Some artillery," Tom Rogers remarked. *Four-deuce* was slang for a 4.2-inch mortar.

"No shit." The smaller weapon spoke first this time. "Looks like our fine feathered friends are serving the Dogs their eviction notice."

Keeping himself flat, McKay risked peeking through the tangled blond hairs of his forearms as the big four-deuce bomb came in. He hadn't heard any splinters rattle around him. He reckoned Soong's mortarmen were firing to a pattern preset months and months ago. He wasn't much concerned about a short round; he didn't know what that madman Andy would do to a crewman who fucked up, but he was sure the crewmen did. And he reckoned he wasn't going to be needing his night vision too much, after all.

There were fires burning in the park, trees tipped every which way in the moonlight. Intermittently McKay could see figures dashing back and forth in the sheer headless-chicken panic that seizes unseasoned troops the first time the steel rain of an artillery barrage falls on their heads. The fuckers were too freaked out even to go to ground, not that that would do them much good. . . .

Thoom. Another eye-melting white sphere, its equator a couple of meters above the ground. Even as its blast was ringing in McKay's ears he heard a strange rippling sound, like a huge deck of cards being shuffled.

"What's that sound?" Sam Sloan asked. The screams redoubled.

"Wood splinters ricocheting off the trees. They're popping in air bursts. Splinters'll do as much damage as blasts and shrapnel."

"Jesus."

CHAPTER
SIX ————————————————

"Will you just fucking look at that," Billy McKay said disbelievingly. "Rice paddies. In the middle of Washington, D.C."

"Maybe mankind's evolving back toward its roots," Sam Sloan observed. "Maybe that's not such a bad thing."

McKay gave him a disbelieving look.

"Welcome to Tide Camp," said their escort, grinning beneath his orderly moustache.

It was three days since the siege of the White House had been unexpectedly lifted by the intervention of Soong's artillery. As promised, next morning the big man himself put in an appearance, walking in through the front gate with a mere handful of retainers: dark, intense Andy trotting at his side, as pumped with nervous energy as a whippet, and a few advisor types who looked like real human beings.

Even McKay had to admit that Soong, his vast body stuffed into a plain olive-drab uniform with captain's bars at his collar and an unmarked baseball-style cap on his head, had cut a hell of an impressive figure. There was something about the man, a presence, a power—he couldn't put his finger on it. And he was not at all sure how it squared with the utterly crazy scene he and Sloan had stumbled onto that first night.

For all his intentions—and those of the rest of the Guardians—to crack down and get right on with the work of settling Jeff MacGregor securely into his once and future seat of government, the Guardians had spent the intervening two days doing a whole hell of a lot of nothing. Even though Sam Sloan shared McKay's doubts about Soong's bunch, there'd been no tactful way to protest when a desperate-looking crew in paint and feathers and cammie pants arrived and began to take up defensive positions outside the White House. They just had no choice but to trust their peculiar allies for now, and even McKay had to admit that by virtue of sheer numbers they were better qualified to protect the President than the Guardians unaided.

And Tom Rogers insisted that Soong was trustworthy. Now that Major Crenna was gone, Tom was perhaps the one man in the world whose judgment Billy McKay would even consider putting a higher value on than his own.

There was still a certain amount of debate that afternoon after Soong left and his squad moved in, but what McKay did was sack out, and for twenty-three uninterrupted hours slept the sleep of the just—the just exhausted.

After that he got up, showered in water stored in

special cisterns beneath the foundation and heated with electricity off the solar accumulators, ate three whole freeze-dried meal packs from Mobile One's store, and went back to bed. As far as he could tell, his buddies did the same. Even hard-core heroes have their breaking points, and the Guardians had been stressed pretty near theirs.

Now their faces had lost their gray undertones, their eyes were no longer red-rimmed and sunken back in shadowed sockets; they stepped out smartly and their skin seemed to fit right again. It was time to get back to work.

First on the agenda was taking stock of their situation—which required taking stock of their new allies' situation. This was the sort of job that old cadreman Rogers did best. As a Special Forces trooper he had dealt with self-proclaimed freedom fighters in most of the obscure crannies of the globe, from genuine patriots through middle-class urban fugitives with blistered feet and jumpy trigger fingers to out-and-out bandits. He was a master at evaluating the strengths and weaknesses of potential allies, figuring out ways to work with them and get things done without offending them or letting them run amok. But as the boss it was McKay's job to scope the place out first. And it was just natural to take Sam Sloan, whose inborn talent for diplomacy had been honed fine by his training at Annapolis, along as a safety rod. If McKay ran into that little puke Andy again, he was going to need one.

"We're quite proud of what we're doing here," their guide said. "It's not everyone who can produce fresh food in the middle of a major metropolitan area."

Sam Sloan nodded agreement. He was an old farm boy from the Ozark country of Missouri. McKay was an inner-city youth from Pittsburgh, vaguely suspicious of anything green and growing. Nevertheless, he could appreciate that the residents of Tide Camp were making some good moves toward survival.

What he was having trouble dealing with were the people bent over with black mud smeared up their shins, working mucky plots around the edge of the Tidal Basin where the Akebono cherry trees used to blossom. They were uniformly small and slight and chattered to one another as they plucked up small green shoots in a language McKay didn't understand any more than he understood what they were doing out there. And they all wore these flat cone-shaped hats woven of straw.

"Just who are these people, anyway?" he asked.

Their guide smiled. He was a black man on the tall side, five foot eleven perhaps, slender built, mid-thirties. Despite the heat of the hazy-white day, he was wearing a suit. Three-piece, neat blue with trim pin-stripes. And a silk tie. His name was Eli Scott, and he seemed to be Soong's chief administrative aide.

"Ethnic Chinese refugees from all over Southeast Asia," he explained. "Thais, Burmese, Nungs from Vietnam, even some from the Philippines and Indonesia. As you gentlemen are no doubt aware, people of Chinese stock enjoy the same status in Asia, outside their own country, as the Jews did in Germany in 1936. What with the worldwide economic slump that preceded the One-Day War, persecution of them increased over the last few years. So large numbers of them came over here."

"Where large numbers of us tried to keep them out," Sam Sloan remarked.

Scott nodded. "Including no few of my own people, I'm ashamed to say."

"Where'd they find them?" McKay asked.

Scott shrugged. "To tell you the truth, I'm not really sure. I think a number were living in a refugee camp in Virginia just before the War. Which still leaves the mystery of how they got from there to here. They just seem to gravitate naturally in this direction; even today we'll have Asiatics wandering in by twos and threes, and not just Chinese. A lot of different sorts of people, actually. Soong is like that. A magnetic sort of man."

His eyes glowed as he spoke. Sam and McKay exchanged glances. As far as they were concerned, Soong had attracted some mighty peculiar types of people.

To McKay's astonishment, Sam Sloan said just that. "I don't mean any offense, Mr. Scott, but that little ceremony the night we arrived took me pretty well aback. Just who are those people, and why does Mr. Soong surround himself with them?"

Scott looked away, obviously flustered. "Boys will be boys, Mr. Sloan. They're mostly harmless."

McKay grunted. He knew he'd felt as if he'd wandered into a bad adventure movie, to the part where spear-carrying natives had caught the intrepid white explorers somewhere in darkest Africa and were just about to tie them to poles and start piling dry brush around them. Even he knew that wasn't going to be a very tactful thing to say to Mr. Scott, however.

"Forgive me, but they didn't seem any too harmless," Sam Sloan said. "Just who are they, and what's the reason for their fanciful costume?"

"You gentlemen will no doubt appreciate the necessity for strong defenses for a settlement such as ours," Scott said obliquely. "To meet that need we have created, in effect, a professional warrior caste."

"*Morani*," Sloan said. It was a Swahili word for a fledged warrior. Scott raised an eyebrow at him momentarily, then went on.

"As to where they come from—they're former police officers and agents of various sorts, FBI, Secret Service, DEA, and so on."

"I thought you were from the Secret Service, Mr. Scott," Sloan said.

"I am. Or rather was. But I was involved more in the investigative end than in enforcement. I specialized in counterfeiting. Most of our, ah, warriors were active enforcement types, and most of them have some kind of background in special military operations."

"I got a background in special operations, too," McKay said, "and I don't go around painting myself up like a goddamned Comanche."

They were walking around the basin, past paddle boats bobbing forlorn and neglected. Scott halted on a rise of ground with his back to a few surviving Yoshino cherry trees, stood with his hands on hips hiking the tails of his coat out to the side with highlights of reflected sun rippling across his face.

"I don't know how familiar either of you gentlemen are with law-enforcement agencies. Most of the men you work with are fine men, committed men." McKay blew a skeptical breath out flared nostrils. He'd gotten a distrust of cops ground into him along with the grime of the Pittsburgh streets. "And the people Soong has gathered for a fighting force are fine men too. But they're of a certain type. Law-enforcement agencies often attract people in what can only be described as a protracted state of adolescence. They're locked in a sort of locker-room mentality, and they have their own rituals, their own ways of doings things."

"Jocks," Sam Sloan said.

"Precisely. So their . . . affectations . . . are reminiscent of those of a fraternity. It helps them maintain their esprit de corps. And they've served us well, Mr. Sloan, very well indeed."

For a moment they stood in uncomfortable silence, broken only by the conversation from the paddies and the cries of gulls circling overhead. "What about that little sawed-off son of a bitch Andy?" McKay demanded. Sloan gave him the old narrow-eye. Well fuck it; he was no goddamned ambassador.

Scott's eyes slid left and right as if to ensure there was no one within overhearing distance. "Lieutenant Aramyan. He served under Soong's command on the Chief's last mission into Cambodia. He saved Soong's life. A brilliant man, in his own way, and courageous, totally without fear, but . . . erratic. Only a little, nothing serious—I'm not criticizing him, you understand. But he is quick-tempered, and I sincerely hope you gentlemen will take that into consideration when dealing with him."

It seemed to McKay that Scott's face had lost its dark gloss and begun to look as if he were rubbing wood ash on himself to help his complexion. "Sooner or later somebody's going to have to kill that little fuck," McKay subvocalized to Sloan.

"Jesus, McKay, don't you start getting caught up in this macho bullshit," Sloan shot back.

Scott shook himself. "Well. Shall I show you the rest of our little community?"

Scott led them across a bridge made of boards supported by air-filled oil drums that spanned the neck of the Washington Channel where it ran into the Tidal Basin. The piers of the former Highway One Bridge, which had been dropped by the succession of hydrogen blasts, stood in the water like silent guardians. The boards and barrels bumped and boomed hollowly beneath their feet.

The island of East Potomac Park almost supported an illusion of normality. Trees and grass appeared as well tended as if the National Park Service were still on the job. Off to the right a couple of hundred meters loomed the pseudo-classical facade of the Jefferson Memorial. They made their way beneath the tangle of interchanges leading to the bridges across the Potomac, which were also down, like all the bridges on the Potomac and the Anacostia from the Woodrow Wilson Bridge clear up to the Beltway Bridge in Montgomery County to the west and the municipality of Brentwood in the east. The tangle of cement Stroganoff noodles had to some extent been cleared of derelict cars, a massive undertaking for the proud survivors of Tide Camp.

As they moved south, McKay could see more rice paddies along the Washington Channel. On the Potomac side of the island double-blossom cherry trees still lined Ohio Drive, more fortunate than their cousins around the basin. There were a few park buildings that had obviously been taken over by the survivors, but the lower half of the island, once a pampered golf course, had become a kind of well-ordered shantytown of what looked to be several hundred small living structures, some tents, but mostly neat square shacks built of scavenged materials, lumber and tarpaper and pressboard.

Walking into the village Scott exchanged friendly greetings with a group stuccoing the wall of what looked like a two-room dwelling. The work gang consisted of about half Asiatics, half young men and women of various races, black, white, Hispanic, dressed for hard work but by no means shabby. They had been laughing and talking among each other cheerfully enough, but McKay noticed that they quieted down noticeably at the sight of the two uniformed men.

"It's really fantastic what you've accomplished here," Sam Sloan said.

"Soong's a great man," Scott said with a smile. He nodded toward another hut, identical to the rest, solidly built but unfinished looking, perched on a low rise on the eastern end of the village. "That's where *he* lives."

"All you people live in these hootches?" McKay asked.

"Most of them. Farmers, workers, families."

"Most of them?" Sloan asked. "What about the soldiers?"

A quick shrug. "Mostly they camp up around the Jefferson Memorial, or around the Basin."

The southern tip of the island reverted to green park once again. McKay and Sloan stood on Hains Point with the perpetual breeze blowing on their faces, Eli Scott proudly erect behind them, and McKay could see that the obvious, unqualified admiration these people displayed for their leader had a solid foundation to it. But as he watched a couple of dozen kids chasing each other with happy screams across the rolling park and splashing in the shallows, he still felt a hard cold ball of doubt down deep in his gut.

CHAPTER
SEVEN ─────────────

"There're a number of major factions within the District of Columbia," the blond man said, tapping a wall-sized LCD color screen that displayed a map of the urban area, "and innumerable smaller groups."

Sam Sloan felt an incredible wave of nostalgia. They were in what had been a war room underneath the White House. Sam had been here before. It was the room in which he, his comrades, then Vice President MacGregor, and Chief Justice Shaneyfelt of the Supreme Court had sat out the thermonuclear bombardment. Aside from the fact that it was stale and close from too many sweating bodies packed into an unventilated room—solar accumulators didn't provide enough power to be used except for emergencies, or for important details such as the display map—it was much the same as it had been back then.

Just as they had then, the four Guardians sat or stood around the table in their characteristic poses: Sam relaxed; Tom Rogers across from him sitting with rigid erectness without apparent effort, as if he were made that way; Casey Wilson slouched bonelessly at the foot of the table; McKay standing over by one wall with his arms folded across his chest, his sleeves rolled up over tree-trunk forearms. Neither Soong nor MacGregor was attending this strategy meeting, but several of the Tide Camp's military leaders were there, unfortunately including Andy Aramyan, hovering off to one side in his own hyper way.

And Bill Madden, who was poking at the street map with one of those silver pointers that telescoped out of a ballpoint pen. Madden looked a little bit like a fuller-faced Nick Nolte, more back than leg, with linebacker shoulders. He had on green army fatigues without rank badges. He was an old war buddy of Billy McKay's, had served with him in Studies and Observations Group, Southwest Asia Command: SOG-SWAC, the dirty-tricks force that operated in support of conventional warfare units in the southern Med during the turbulent years before the War.

Their reunion had been enthusiastic, with much arm-punching and back-slapping and promises to get together and get shitfaced on salvaged beer as soon as possible, and McKay had announced that he felt a whole hell of a lot better about this outfit if it had his ol' buddy Bill attached to it. *He* wasn't one of the goofballs who dressed like something off MTV. But Sloan wondered if ol' Bill didn't sometimes put aside his OD's for war paint and feathers himself.

"Of the big-leaguers, we've got the Georgetown Boys to the northwest of us and Rushton's American Union people practically on the doorstep, over to the Hill. Rushton makes a lot of noise, but he's mostly talk. Over east of him on both sides of the Anacostia you've got

Jabbar and his crew. They're blacks, into some pretty radical politics. Up north along Rock Creek Park—"

" 'Scuse me," Sam Sloan interjected, "but that wouldn't be Malcolm Jabbar, by any chance?"

Madden's chin bobbed. "Sure would."

"What are you talking about now?" McKay grunted.

"He was a fairly important black political leader back before the War," Sloan explained. "Headed up a group called Spectrum. It was supposed to be an alliance of people of all races to work for social justice." He frowned. "I have to admit, Jabbar was a pretty peculiar choice to lead it. Some pretty rough quotes were attributed to him in the press. Anti-Semitism, stuff like that. He always denied it, claimed media persecution, but it happened enough to make you wonder."

McKay rubbed his jaw and in the still dead air Sloan could hear the rasp of stubble. "Huh. Another puke."

Sloan felt a rush of irritation. Here was a political leader of some importance, and Billy McKay was just dismissing him out of hand with a crudity. Sometimes he didn't know what to make of the Guardians' leader.

"I don't know if I'd exactly call him a radical. He was never on very good terms with the far-left black groups," he said.

Madden shrugged. "Well, political anyway. Up by the park we've got another black political type from before the War, guy named McDaniels. His outfit's called the Gold Coast. Then you got the smaller fry, like the Super Machos up around Columbia Road—they're mostly Puerto Rican—the Nuclear Winners, the Bloods, the Rangers, the Warlords."

"Or the Red Dog Family?" Casey asked.

Andy Aramyan yipped a short laugh. "Like they used to be. They didn't stop running yet."

"Finally, you got the straight-out scum, the bandit

gangs: the Rebel Runners, the Death Commandos, the Pagans, the Pirates. There's no keeping track of them, they come and go all the time, or wipe each other out."

"What contacts you got with these groups?" Tom Rogers wanted to know.

Madden hesitated.

"Contacts?" Andy said. He laughed. "They don't fuck with us. If they do, we teach 'em better. That's our contacts."

Bill Madden fitted Sam Sloan's definition of a hard-ass pretty thoroughly, but that was a bit much even for him. "We have a kind of *modus vivendi* with the larger factions. The rest—well, it's just like Andy says."

"You don't, like, trade with any of the other groups?" asked Casey.

Andy snorted through dilated nostrils.

"Our civilians deal at the Rubble Mart some, up in Northwest by the Maryland line," Madden said guardedly. "Nothing major."

"It might be time we started," Sam Sloan said. "Surely you can't fulfill all your people's needs simply with what you've done around Tide Camp, no matter how impressive."

All of a sudden he wasn't missing the air conditioning so much; the room's temperature had plummeted. Soong's people were giving him some pretty hard glares.

"We scavenge, just like everybody else," said a small Hispanic named Olmeida. "There's plenty out there for us to get by."

That was true enough, Sloan knew. The blast and heat and radiation effects of the bombs were tougher on humans than on, say, canned goods, or mechanical equipment; fallout didn't hurt artifacts at all. Nor had there been a protracted period of wartime shortages. After the all-clear sounded a million corpses were rotting in the hot summer sun and the torrential rain with which it alternated, breeding every disease known to humankind in glorious profusion.

Later, after the bodies rotted out and the fallout faded, survivors began to drift back in, drawn by the lure of tons of loot buried in the rubble or just sitting in less damaged buildings. It was a pattern repeated in most major population centers to a greater or lesser extent, particularly in the heavily pounded urban sprawl of the Eastern Seaboard.

"We'd be obliged if you could help us make contact with the heads of these other factions," Rogers said.

Everybody stared at him. "What do you mean?" somebody else asked. "You're not seriously thinking of dealing with these fuckers?"

"Like it or not," Sloan said, "we all have to live together in what remains of this city."

Suddenly Andy Aramyan was standing right in front of him, fists clenched at his hips, shouting down into his face. "You saying we're shit? You saying we can't take care of ourselves? We kept this place for you like a shrine, a year we kept it. What are you saying, we can't hang on to it?"

Growling, McKay pushed himself away from the wall. Sloan felt a massive spill of anger inside him, which froze his face and tone of voice. "I'm not impugning your people in any way, Mr. Aramyan. But the situation has changed. Surely you have to acknowledge that fact."

"Yeah," Olmeida scoffed. "You fancy boys come waltzing in here in your funny car and think you got the right to boss us around."

For a moment Sloan feared McKay would take a swing at the guy. Every man in the room was armed with at least a pistol and a knife apiece—no amount of diplomacy had convinced Soong's warriors to check their hardware at the White House door, and they'd reacted violently enough to the suggestion that not even McKay felt like forcing the issue. At the same instant that Sam felt ashamed for losing control of the situation, he was very glad McKay insisted his own people go armed at all times no matter how secure things seemed.

"Let's just everybody back off and talk reasonable." It was Tom Rogers, the only man in the room apparently untouched by the sudden tension. Even laid-back Casey had his feet on the floor and his muscles yanked taut, but Tom just sat there as rock-steady and effortless as before, and looked at them all with steady gray eyes. "We got a misunderstanding. Let's talk about it."

The tension burst like a floating soap bubble. Rogers had that ability; it had to be his calm certainty. Only Andy glared at him a minute longer, and then his shoulder slumped and he shook his head and muttered something under his breath. Sloan wondered if it were just one of his mercurial mood changes, or if he'd just gotten smart.

Not that the Armenian would have been risking anything by shouting at his former SF colleague. In the three years of their acquaintance, Sam Sloan had never known any amount of verbal abuse to shift Tom Rogers one micron off center. If, on the other hand, Tom Rogers decided that Andy or any other human being needed to be dead, then that person was *gone* with mechanical precision and no more compunction than a great white shark shows.

The Guardians were by definition pretty tough hombres, but it had taken Sam Sloan—who'd had a pretty sheltered life, even though he was a shrewd judge of character—a year to realize that the unassuming, almost colorless Rogers was beyond question the toughest man he'd ever known or ever would. Even McKay, whose swaggering, loud-mouthed exterior concealed one genuinely mean son of a bitch, admitted point-blank that he'd hate to go up against Tom Rogers. Sam liked Tom, would—and had—trusted him with his life. But he could never be a hundred percent comfortable with him.

"We 'preciate everything you've done," Tom Rogers said. "It's taken a lot of faith and courage to preserve the White House for when the President came back. But now the President is back, and he's going to be working on rebuilding the nation—with your help and ours—from right here. Everybody's gonna have enough work to do without spending all our time holding off attacks. That's why we need to try to work out some kind of understanding with the other groups hereabouts."

There was something about the way he said *understanding* that made it clear that it was just as likely to be an understanding based on fear of certain reprisal as any kind of friendship. It was one of the things the Tide People wanted to hear, if not exactly everything.

As people eased back and hands left weapon butts, Sloan sat forward, intrigued. It was as many words as he'd ever heard Rogers string together before. He knew Rogers was an expert cadreman, skilled in dealing with touchy and unreliable allies. But he'd never seen the former Green Beret exercise that skill before. Always before when Rogers had done such work as a Guardian the group had been split up, organizing a guerrilla campaign against the Church of the New Dispensation in Colorado, or the much more ambitious rabble-rousing program that led up to the climactic assault on the Heartland. It was clear the locals weren't exactly happy with what the Guardians were proposing, but neither were they ready to bolt—or go for their guns.

"Besides," Tom Rogers said with a sliver of a smile,

"maybe some folks will start pushing a bit harder, now the President's here."

Sam Sloan didn't know just how prophetic those words were.

The meeting ended amicably enough, but the Guardians had the feeling the issue was a long way from settled. Their suspicion was confirmed that night when Soong himself arrived to call upon President MacGregor.

For a wonder Andy Aramyan wasn't along, and the gigantic Secret Service agent was accompanied only by a pair of skinny-shanked Vietnamese with Belgian FNCs slung around their necks, who squatted on the South Portico in the evening gloom and smoked while their boss went inside.

Servants from Tide Camp were at work in the White House kitchens, preparing dinner. Others were at work cleaning up broken glass, mildewed paper, the occasional human bone, and other debris from the blasts and the past year as Sam Sloan escorted Soong to the Lincoln Suite on the second floor, which MacGregor was using for an office. Aside from the fact that the President's usual offices in the West Wing had sustained more damage than the White House proper, McKay refused to clear either wing for use by the President. Even with Soong's people walking perimeter patrol they were just too vulnerable to attack from the street or the buildings across—and McKay still wasn't altogether sure of Soong's gunslingers either. He was uncomfortable having the White House full of Tide Camp people, but he realized there was just no choice; as the adventure with the Red Dog Family had proved, there really weren't enough Guardians to defend the White House adequately, much less clear out the crap.

Besides, finding he had as yet no Blueprint-connected work to do, Dr. Srinarampa had of his own accord donned rough work clothes and joined with a will in the crews cleaning up the place. The plump little doctor might have been pisspoor in a fight, but he was sharp and keen-eyed, and McKay felt a little better with him keeping tabs on the Tide Camp work crews.

Upstairs Jeff MacGregor was at work behind an open door, studying printouts from the White House's operational computers—some had been built around silicon-lattice semiconductors, and had survived the electromagnetic pulses of Soviet warheads. He wasn't liking what he saw. He hoped to move part, if not all, of the assembled Blueprint people—who had been left for safekeeping in the Iowa town of Luxor, which the Guardians had liberated from the renegade National Guardsmen mere days after the War—into Washington to resume the work of rebuilding America. Much of their labor, along with the data base containing every-thing that had been pieced together about the lost Blueprint itself, had unavoidably been destroyed with Heartland. It was vital that it be recovered as soon as possible. But the prognosis wasn't promising.

Soong bowed in the doorway as Sloan discreetly withdrew. "A few words with you, Mr. President?"

Wearily, MacGregor nodded. "Please come in, Mr. Soong." He rested his elbows on the desk top and massaged his temples. "Will you have a seat?"

Soong nodded graciously and settled his bulk into a leather-and-chrome swivel chair dragged in from the West Wing. It didn't fit the decor. He was wearing a blue silk robe and sandals, his usual costume. "I believe there was some disagreement between your men and mine about handling the various factions that occupy the rubble of Washington."

"So I understand."

"I'm afraid I have to convey a certain dissatisfaction on the part of my men. They feel that by their long vigil they have earned the sole right to act as your bodyguards. They don't take lightly to being given orders by men they regard as . . . interlopers."

"You mean they resent the Guardians?" MacGregor asked, more testily than he intended.

Gravely, Soong nodded. "It pains me to say so, Mr. President. But they feel the Guardians have served their purpose in bringing you here, and it is time they withdraw to other chores, or join with my own people—where their talents would, I assure you, be appreciated."

MacGregor stared hard at him. He remembered Soong from the days he had just been another face on the rotating White House security detail, and he'd been impossible to read even then. Now, as the apparently benevolent potentate of his mini-kingdom in Southwest Washington, D.C., the man was more of an enigma than ever. MacGregor was grateful for what Soong and his people had done, but there was something about the single-minded devotion they displayed that unsettled him.

"I can sympathize with your men's feelings, Mr. Soong. But I'm afraid that what they're asking for just simply isn't feasible. The Guardians got me out of Washington after the One-Day War, and they returned me here. They were specifically assembled and trained as an elite Presidential guard." *One that understandably aroused the resentment of a lot of Secret Service men,* he remembered. "As a former Special Forces officer and senior agent of the Secret Service, surely you are aware—more so than I—of the nature of elite formations. The Guardians regard ensuring my security as their mission, and nothing except success or death is going to budge them an inch."

He leaned forward. "Besides, Mr. Soong, they weren't merely throwing their weight around this afternoon. We need to get Project Blueprint up and running, which means bringing in as many Blueprint personnel as possible, as soon as possible. And according to these figures"—he tapped the printout with his fingertips—"we haven't the food, or facilities to house them, much less permit them actually to get back on the job of coordinating America's recovery. Washington must be secured, Mr. Soong. And not even the combined talents of your men and mine can take the entire city by conquest."

Soong nodded again. "That is true."

For a time they sat in silence while the darkness fell around them. Always energy conscious, MacGregor delayed turning on the accumulator-powered lights as long as he could.

"I will convey your message to my men," Soong said finally. "It is no more than they expected. But I fear they may insist on a condition of their own."

MacGregor looked at him.

"You have found the Guardians invaluable protectors, Mr. President. But my men know nothing of them beyond what they read in press releases before the War. Some, indeed, recall that the Guardians fled in the safety of armored personnel carriers while their own comrades were left to face the mobs and die. Wait—" He held up a huge broad hand to ward off the anger he saw clamping down on MacGregor's handsome features. "Forgive me, Mr. President, I am only telling you what certain people believe; I know that it is groundless, but men take the deaths of comrades-in-arms hard, not always reasonably.

"My men are loyal to me, as yours are to you, but even such loyalty as theirs has limits. They will only consent to serve alongside the Guardians if the Guardians prove themselves in action."

MacGregor half rose. "The Guardians have proved themselves over and over, in actions all across the United States of America—"

Unperturbed, Soong nodded again, smiling a vague troubled smile. "True, Mr. President," he said, "but not in front of my men. And that they must do."

CHAPTER
EIGHT ────────────────────────

The chance wasn't long in coming.

Billy McKay was awakened a little after 0800 by a squelch from his personal communicator, which was sitting on the bedside table in the third-floor room he'd appropriated for his quarters. McKay was not a man to rise early of his own accord. Since at the moment the Guardians were on more or less stand-down status he was sleeping as much as he felt like. And that was a lot. There was a limit to endurance no matter how tough a man is, and by rights the Guardians had passed theirs weeks since.

He rolled over and dropped one hand to the butt of the .45 tucked between the mattress and the box springs. With the other he hit the button on the communicator.

"McKay. What is it?" he asked blearily.

"Sloan. We've got problems."

"How urgent?" It was no emergency, he already knew from Sam's tone. Except when he was negotiating, Sam didn't have much of a poker voice.

"Not much."

"Down in ten."

Late riser or not, McKay was showered and shaved and crisply uniformed when he trotted down the stairs, his short blond hair wet-dark and combed back sleek along his skull.

"You look like something out of a George Raft movie," Sloan said as he came into the foyer.

Sloan was still wearing his blue-and-white Adidas running suit. Stand-down or not, McKay thought irritably, he'd undoubtedly been up at the crack of goddamn dawn and running up to Baltimore and back for a little wake-up exercise. Actually, McKay was unsure where Sloan had found to run that was anywhere near secure, unless he'd run fifteen or twenty times around the South Lawn. He noted approvingly that Sloan was wearing his Colt .357 Magnum Python in its shoulder holster over the running suit, even though McKay hated the chromed pistol's shininess.

"Cute. What's going on?" he asked.

"Our friend Andy has come to visit and brighten our morning. And he has someone with him."

Soong's right-hand man was waiting for them in the foyer to the South Portico. A wizened Vietnamese woman stood by one side, belt-buckle-high and distraught. She had her sinewy brown hands up to her face and was crying loudly in between ragged chunks of Vietnamese. Tom Rogers stood beside her, trying to soothe her in a low voice. He spoke a fair amount of the language from his own time on the ground in Southeast Asia.

"Good morning, boys." Aramyan was poised so far forward on the balls of his feet that McKay expected he'd pitch on over and bounce his chin off the carpet if he took one step. He wore a taut little grin, but his black brows were pulled together tight. "The Captain told you we wanted you to prove yourselves. Now you got the chance."

"I can hardly wait," McKay said.

"We lost a couple kids. Early this morning."

"Killed?" Sloan asked with a pitying look at the woman.

A quick head shake. "Negative. Taken. Out foraging—hunting."

He paused, rocking slightly, grinning, waiting for the Guardians to evince surprise. He was doomed to disappointment. The Guardians had received the fullest and best briefings on survival after the holocaust available anywhere as part of their training. They were hip to what the kidnapped youths had been up to.

Surprising as it sounds, any urban area, even the hugest megalopolis, swarms with small game. From pigeons and rats, to cats and dogs run wild after the War, the city was a rich source of nourishment if you weren't squeamish. The squeamish didn't last long, here in the ruins.

So, "Right," McKay said without batting an eye. "Who got them?"

"Little no-name bunch of crazies. So bad no gang will have them. They give us trouble one, two months now. Never enough for us to go clean 'em out."

"Until now," Sloan said.

Aramyan grinned.

"What happened?" Sam Sloan asked. "Just who did they take?"

"Boy and a girl, the boy seventeen, the girl fifteen or so. Out with a group of six, eight others. These two were paired up—we work on the buddy system, and these two were always going buddies, okay? Apparently these assholes jumped them. The other kids were nearby, heard screams, and a couple of shots from little .22 rifles the kids were carrying. They found some blood. Don't know whose, but our kids can take care of themselves.''

"This lady lose her daughter?" McKay asked.

"Her son, Billy," Rogers said.

"Girl's a refugee from Maryland. Wandered in last fall.''

"Why do you think they took them?" Sloan asked.

Andy shrugged. "Who knows? Hostage, torture, rape. Eat 'em, maybe."

Sloan shot a horrified look at the woman. Andy laughed. "No fear, bro. She don't understand English.''

"So did these scumbags leave some kind of trail the kids could follow?"

"Oh, yeah. Our kids are sharp; they got good eyes. But they know not to follow. Even lowlives like these got Uzis, M-16s, that shit. Armories all over the city.''

"Fucking great." McKay took the first cigar of the morning from a breast pocket, crackled off the age-dried cellophane wrapper, sniffed it. It had not aged well; smelled like shredded cardboard. What the fuck, over. It was salvage, a gift from Soong himself. Ignoring Sam's expression of distaste, he bit off the end, stuck it in his face, flipped out a butane lighter, and lit up.

"Can we borrow one of these kids to show us the trail? If a man laid it, Tommy can follow it," he asked.

Andy chuckled. "Shit, don't worry about that. We know where they are. Take you right there." That smile again, slashing like a saber. "Like I told you, it was just never worth the trouble to take them out before.''

"So how about it, Billy?" Casey asked. "Do we wait for nightfall?"

McKay heard Andy suck in breath, guessed he'd been hoping for just such a question, decided to body-check him. "Negative. Since we don't know what the assholes took the kids for, we don't know how long they'll keep them alive, especially if the dink kid punctured one of them. Let's saddle up and go."

The Guardians lounged in lawn chairs on the South Portico, squinting into the sun and haze and waiting for the team of Soong's—or Aramyan's—men who would guide them to the vicinity of their objective.

"Shit." McKay shook his head. "I can't make that dude at all. He came on all strong and hostile, but then just before he took off it was like he was really concerned about us coming back okay. Like we were all related to him or something."

"You don't think he was acting?" Sloan said.

"Negative. It may seem crazy, but it felt like he meant it."

"It sure doesn't tally very well with his reaction to us before," Sloan said.

"Yeah, like he's schizophrenic or something."

A half-dozen men came out of the Ellipse on foot. They were a wild-looking bunch, all but one bare-chested, all bristling with guns and fetishes. It amazed Billy that such a gang of obvious assholes contained a high proportion of special-missions soldiers, some of them not much less case-hardened than the Guardians themselves. Soong, or his gray eminence, as Sloan called Andy, exercised some pretty keen judgment in picking his shock troops. The sense of unity they were building for themselves was something else again.

"They don't act like most people I've run across who've just lost friends or loved ones to bandits," Sloan remarked as they strolled across the cratered South Lawn. "Usually they're uptight. Quietly intense or boisterous—but uptight, just the same."

"I don't think that, like, these guys identify too much with the rest of Tide Camp," Casey observed, lounging back with his legs crossed and his back up against a fluted pillar.

Sam winced. "Sheepdogs and sheep," he muttered.

"Ready for some huntin'?" called the apparent leader of the approaching group.

Sloan stood. "I prefer to think of it as an errand of mercy, myself."

The newcomers laughed.

They moved out together around the West Wing and up through Lafayette Park. The park was a mess. The four-deuce mortar had snapped off half the trees at chest height, scattering kindling over the trampled grass around the battered statue of Andy Jackson on his horse.

At least old Andy was still up on his hobbyhorse. The other four equestrian statues, spotted on the corners, were toppled. McKay sketched a salute to one.

"Friend of yours?" Tide Camp squad leader Tyler asked.

"Ancestor, if you believe the polack side of my family. Thaddeus Kosciusko."

"Son of a bitch."

"Yeah, he was." McKay grinned. "Say it runs in the family."

Recognizable here and there were the blackened fairy rings of campfires past, a few shredded tents, colorful scraps of candy wrappers and food cans. Here and there a booted foot kicked up a clump of cloth thick with crusty brown stains—all that was left of the Red Dog Family after Soong's bombardment and subsequent mopping-up. Soong's people had policed up everything of any value, which for the Third World peasants among them was just about anything larger than a matchstick. They had also policed up the bodies, thank God. The whole park stank of death anyway.

Once they were through the mood lightened. The Tide Camp commandos began smoking and joking with the Guardians, even though they were crossing over into Indian country. It wasn't unprofessional; they were trying to maintain a casual, business-as-usual profile to avoid alerting the raiders.

"So tell me," McKay said around his cigar, "just why the hell do you guys do yourself up in all that funky shit, anyway?"

The question had an edge to it, a backing of steel. These were not just your random meatballs, goofs and bikers and runners. These were men who were—had been—soldiers, many of whom had seen action. His mind was having trouble making these characters fit that mold, even though little things about them, the way they carried their weapons in the patrol position, relaxed but ready, the way their eyes scanned the blank-faced buildings around even as they shot the shit with apparent casualness, showed these men were no amateurs. McKay didn't know what to make of it.

"Mark of distinction, man," said Tyler. He was a rangy dude with a narrow bony face, the sides of his head shaven, the remaining hair a flat-top bleached to the shade of the white war stripe painted from cheekbone to cheekbone across the bridge of his nose. He wore an open dark blue vest with light blue back, which had once been part of a three-piece suit, cammie gym shorts, Nike running shoes. He carried a Belgian made FN-FAL. "Badge of the warrior, that sort of thing."

"Yeah. Set us off from the sheep," said Langetti, one of the more normal-looking ones of the bunch.

"Ain't you guys taking that a little far?" McKay wanted to know.

"It's nothing new, McKay," Sam said. "Paratroopers wore Mohawks thirty years before the punks and the metalheads found out about it—half century before there *were* road gypsies."

"C'mon, don't shit me," said Martin, a lean black loping along with an M-16–M-203 combination and a necklace that seemed to consist of human finger bones and a cat's skull slung around his neck. "Don't you dudes wish you could really get decked out right and strut your stuff?"

"No." McKay clamped a bulldog jaw on his cigar and scowled.

"You should." It was Rosen, whose black eyes burned holes in a thin ascetic's face coated in thick white pancake. "The warrior is the scapegoat of society—and its savior. He deserves privilege, acknowledgement of his role. That's what *we* get."

"I'm just a simple farm boy," Sloan said. "This is all a bit much for my taste. More like Kerry, over there."

He jutted his chin at the youngest member of the group, a likable, muscular blond kid, Ranger trained, who'd just been accepted for training by the District of Columbia Police Department when the balloon went up. He was one of the few Tide Camp bravos to be openly friendly to the Guardians, hanging around them and asking questions and generally hero-worshiping. Normally he went barechested, the prime mark of distinction, it seemed, for the warriors of Tide Camp. Today he wore a gray University of Maryland sweatshirt, with cracked and eroded white lettering, the elastic neckpiece and arms cut out so it more resembled a mutilated pillowcase than a garment. The young man blushed and bobbed his head.

"Yeah, what's the occasion? Why you all dressed up like that?" McKay wanted to know.

"It's the weather," said Tyler, whose face was already dripping with sweat in the hundred-plus degree heat. "He don't want to catch a chill."

They swung north and vaguely west, not only to avoid following too closely on the marauders' heels and risk running afoul of lookouts watching the backtrail, but also to avoid brushing up against pickets from the gang—or commune, or tribe, or settlement, or whatever—that called itself the Georgetown Boys. There was no love lost between them and Soong's crew.

Even McKay had to admit that the Tide Camp people hadn't done such a hell of a good job of diplomacy. Except for making sure everyone's shit turned to water at the very *thought* of messing with the White House in any way, shape, or form.

The route wasn't easy. Contrary to almost everyone's expectations, Washington hadn't been flashed into a glassy crater by the Soviets during the One-Day War. As the President had definite plans to be elsewhere during a strategic thermonuclear exchange, there weren't really that many hard military targets on hand. And whatever their propaganda might have been saying the week the hammer came down, neither the Soviets nor the Americans had extra warheads to toss at other than high-priority targets—like missile farms and bomber bases.

But that didn't mean Washington got off scot-free. Five warheads had gone off in the area; one, delayed an hour, almost in the footprint of an earlier blast—the latecomer that the Guardians thought had detonated over the Capitol itself, and which destroyed the armored car in which Chief Justice Shaneyfelt was riding. They had pretty well kicked the stuffing out of the city.

This central section of the District proper, north from the vicinity of the White House along Sixteenth Street, was the least damaged part of the city. None of the explosions had gone off near enough for this strip to lie within their primary- or secondary-blast, or even thermal-effects, zones. But their fringes had overlapped, producing patterns of destruction that were quirky even by the standards of nuclear blasts.

In one place a block of buildings would be standing apparently intact, with only the glass blown out and not even the paint blistered, and the next block would look as if someone had scraped it level with a gigantic knife. The party was making pretty good time, moving fast and loose with one of the Tide Camp people on point, strung out in a loose vee formation. They were not trying to be particularly covert. Infiltrating a built-up urban area—even one that's rubbled and mostly deserted —in broad daylight isn't the easiest of tasks. The Guardians could have done it, no problem—if they'd had a day or so to get into position. Aramyan's mission briefing to them had indicated that time was of the essence.

The idea was to work up to a point due east of the bandits' hideout, then close in from that direction. At that point they'd break company with their escorts. Aside from the fact that good ol' Andy had made abundantly clear that the Guardians had to do this on their own, with no support at all from Tide Camp—including the secretly sited mortars—nobody wanted to chance the bad guys spotting people in distinctive Tide Camp drag moving in on them.

Oddly enough, the raiders would almost certainly not find a party of four heavily armed men, even dressed in the Guardians' distinctive urban-warfare camouflage with its cubist patterns of black and gray and white, too threatening. In the rubble, everyone went armed. And cammie suits of every description imaginable were available in derelict sporting goods stores or blown-open arsenals. Spotting the Guardians on their turf would make their targets wary, but they wouldn't instantly realize that this visit was personal.

Just north of Logan Circle the Guardians and their escort were crossing an exposed area, where the buildings to the east were gone into rain-smoothed mounds of rubble and the ones to the west had mostly been shaved off a meter or so into the second story, when a shot spanged off a rusted joint of pipe, which jutted like a compound fracture from a pile of debris to the left, and *screed* off down the street. Before the sound of the shot proper had reached their ears the Guardians were one with the debris underfoot, rooting for cover with guns at the ready.

Billy Mckay found himself behind a half-buried armchair of tasteful orange plastic. He spit ashy-tasting grit out of his mouth around the butt of his cigar, which had gone out when he'd gone down. As he squinted out through the molten sunlight, he heartily wished for a weapon with more range and authority than the stubby little MP-5 submachine gun he was presently carrying. Then he looked up and noticed the Tide Camp troopies standing around looking down at him with these shit-eating grins hanging off their faces.

"What the fuck are you staring at?"

"Little dry for swimming," Tyler drawled.

"Shit. You dudes just too wound up," Martin offered. "You spend enough time screwing around in this rubble, you get used to being shot at."

"If your response is to stand around flat-footed like

that," Sloan said tartly, "I take it you're used to getting hit a lot too."

They laughed. "Scrub who busted that cap's long gone," Tyler remarked. "Nothing personal. People in this shit heap like to loose a round now and again at somebody just to remind themselves they're human."

They were belly down in the wreckage of some tavern, squinting into heat haze that hung low on the streets and shimmered in bright pools on car backs and starred windshields.

"They got their bolt-hole thirteen hundred meters or so due west of here, couple of blocks past the Hilton." Tyler was giving them a final briefing. "Walk careful around the Hilton. Folks we're after don't use it—it's just too burned-out for permanent quarters, even for them—but you got a pretty constant transient population."

"Transients with guns," Sloan commented.

"Fuckin'-A straight. In your modern urban environment, even the derelicts got heavy artillery."

"Don't suppose you people'd be willing to lend us a little backup?" McKay asked.

"Nope."

"Then I guess it's up to us hard-core heroes to do the job. Time to haul ass, boys and girls." He hauled himself up out of the rubble.

Sloan slapped young Kerry on the shoulder. "Don't wait up for us." His brow furrowed suddenly. "Say, what's that on your chest? Looks like a burn of some kind—" He reached for the open neck of the young man's sweatshirt.

The boy jerked away as if fearing Sloan's fingers were hot. "I'm okay. Just don't—I mean, I'm okay."

"But it looks as if you've got a pretty nasty little burn

there—cigarette burn, or something. Ought to let Tom look at that.''

"I'm fine." Kerry was sweating even more profusely than the heat of the day could account for.

Sloan shrugged. "If that's the way you're going to be." He stood up. "Let's go."

CHAPTER
NINE ──────────────

The kidnappers' hideout was tucked into a sort of salient formed by a meander of Rock Creek Park and marked off to the east by Connecticut and Florida Avenues. Steering clear of the derelict Hilton, many of whose windows had freakishly survived the overlapping blast waves, so that its face presented a bizarre mosaic, the Guardians infiltrated past the burned-out Boy Scouts headquarters building, making maximum use of cover. Time still pressed, but they judged that the extra minutes it was taking to sneak and peek in the last two hundred meters wouldn't hurt them as much as being spotted by the bad guys.

This was the celebrated Embassy Row district, though the enclave was devoted mostly to Third World embassies, as far as McKay could see, and those of places like Finland and Iceland that weren't in the Third World, but weren't much of anywhere else, either. Right by the apex of the bend in the park, near the

French Embassy (McKay privately thought of France as part of the Third World) sprawled the Islamic Center. It was a focus for nearly constant combat as various factions of Sunni, Shi'ite, and various black American Muslim sects vied for control.

Even now, slipping quietly across a linoleum floor with the blue sky shining right in where the roof used to be, the Guardians could hear the *pop-pop-pop* of small-arms fire in that direction, comfortably distant. No matter. The people over by the mosque had enough to keep themselves amused, and even though the Guardians' quarry were getting pretty daring, they presumably wouldn't have lived over a year since the holocaust by being dumb enough to go poking at gangs of well-armed cranks who probably didn't like white folks much anyway.

In fact the martial Muzak was a potential help to the Guardians. Their quarry would of course have gotten in the habit of tuning out a large portion of background noise. It would make it that much easier to sneak up on them.

They moved silently, hunched over their weapons, scuttling across open streets between mounded fields of debris, moving catlike through ruined buildings. The air was utterly still, and this near the river the humidity was crowding three figures and the temperature was well past.

Sam Sloan, bringing up the rear with a submachine gun slung and a stubby M-79 grenade launcher in his hands—the team's sole bet-hedge against real trouble—paused to mop at his forehead with the cuff of one cubist sleeve. *Imagine a little hike like this wearing you out—an ol' Olympic marathoner like you,* he thought.

Though he was fanatical about fitness, and his teammates, if less obsessive, were no less determined to keep themselves at the peak of physical conditioning their mission required, they'd spent most of last year riding around in their armored car, and it wasn't easy to stay fit that way. But suffering the heat or not they drove on. So did he. They were Guardians.

As they worked their way behind a brownstone facade that stood alone like the false front of a building in a Hollywood backlot Western town—all that remained of the embassy of some postage-stamp Pacific republic—he wondered what his teammates were thinking. Rogers, ghosting on point with his MP-5 poised like an exotic extension of his own body, could have been thinking nothing or anything; Sloan couldn't read him and never expected to.

Next in line McKay, making no more noise than the compact ex-Green Beret despite his football player's bulk, was chewing on the butt of an unlit cigar and frowning around at the world in that half-unconscious way of his, the harsh sunlight turning his pale eyebrows almost white. *He* was probably thinking about where his next cigar would come from, or his next beer—or his next blowjob.

Then Casey, bopping along in his Genesis tour cap and the yellow Zeiss shooting glasses, which McKay would have insisted he take off on the grounds they distorted his vision, had he not been able to see a fly clean its wings at a hundred feet with or without them. His mind was probably locked into some meditation mandala, Sam guessed, or maybe he was daydreaming about being swaddled once more in the high-tech cocoon that was the cockpit of his F-16. Or he could be thinking about one of the gorgeous young women— Rhoda at Balin's Forge, for example, or Angie Connoly back at the Freehold in Colorado—he'd conquered in their travels.

And me? Sloan grinned to himself. *Just poking my mind with a finger to keep it from settling back into the pre-mission willies.* It never did occur to him his buddies were doing the same thing.

"Okay," Billy McKay growled, "we got our answer. These are smart bad guys."

A hundred meters away stood the building they'd been told was the raiders' hideout. If they'd been stupid, this gang would have picked a building in a largely intact block, vastly simplifying the Guardians' problem of terminal approach—over rooftops, through basements, even, if need, through walls, using the specialized explosives distributed among their lightweight backpacks, as well as Tom Rogers's skill. But they hadn't been so accommodating.

The hideout was a nondescript four-story building about two-thirds of the way down the block. It was the only building standing on either side of the street. On the side toward the Guardians it appeared as if the structure next to it had been sheared off clean, as by a giant knife cutting through cake; scarcely more remained of it than a pile of masonry crumbs. What they could see of the other side from this angle looked as if some raggedy remains of a structure clung to its western side, but that was it. There was no cover higher than a rain-eroded pile of wreckage within thirty meters at the closest.

However, west of the solitary structure buildings still stood, and there were some reasonably intact structures on the next block south. Rubbing his chin, McKay nodded to himself. A plan was taking form.

"Just wish I had my hog along," he commented. "I could make some short work of these fuckers."

"But the object is to rescue the captives," Sloan said, "not to saw down the building around their ears." He said it a little tentatively, as if expecting McKay to bite his head off, but the big ex-marine just grinned at him.

They had all left their primary weapons back at the White House. Not just the M-60 whose lack McKay lamented, but Casey's high-tech sniper's rifle, Sam Sloan's Galil-203 combo, even Rogers's Short Assault Rifle. The kind of action they were up against would go down at spitting distance, where the brute shocking power of the .45 slug the silenced German submachine guns fired was more valuable than the capacity to produce tremendous tissue damage—frequently with little immediate effect—of a 5.56 round.

Success hinged on the Guardians shooting first, hitting what they aimed at, and the people they hit going down. For that, shotguns would have been ideal; but even though shotguns didn't throw as all-encompassing a pellet pattern as was popularly believed, they were just too indiscriminate for use in a hostage situation. This was all going to come down to the stubby MP-5s—and side-arms and knives, if it came to that.

Wishing like hell for a beer, McKay outlined his plan to the others. Quick and dirty; no choice. There was no debate.

Under normal circumstances they would have gone to ground in the rubble at least a day in advance, just to watch the comings and goings. But there was no time. They had to *move*.

It was going to cause them problems.

"Billy."

McKay frowned. Sloan hardly ever called him by his first name. "I think we have a problem."

McKay and Rogers lay on their bellies in broken glass in a gutted laundromat on the ground floor of the first building standing west of the hideout. From this vantage point they could see that stumps of all four floors of the structure formerly attached to this side of their objective still jutted like shelves from the side of the building, sporadically supported by crumbling walls. If there was enough structural strength left to support their weight it was almost as good a pathway in as they could have asked for, almost as good as being able to go in over the roof. Provided the kidnappers didn't have the captives right up against one of the west walls on the top floor, the two Guardians could enter there and do a classic top-down housecleaning operation while the bad guys were still wondering what the hell was going on.

Or maybe not. "Go ahead, Sam."

"I'm in position now, a couple of short blocks north. And I can see something we didn't see before."

"Like what?"

"Like about eight of these guys playing basketball in the parking lot."

There was a long silence. Somewhere beyond McKay's boot soles a mouse scooted through the debris. "Just how many men did our good buddy Andy say these scumbags had?" he asked.

"Six or eight, Billy," Tom said by his side.

"Intelligence error?" Sam Sloan's voice asked.

"I fuckin' wonder."

But he didn't; he knew. He was boiling. They had been set up. That much was plain. The only question now was whether they had been sent in expecting only half the opposition they faced to take them down a peg—or whether they were never intended to come back at all.

"Like, what are the chances they're all outside playing?" Casey asked.

McKay just snorted. He was too seriously pissed off even to tease the kid.

There was no time to bitch and moan about it. Overhead the sun was already well past zenith. This little surprise only increased the Guardians' determination to bring back a hundred percent success from this mission—and then stuff Andy Aramyan's boot up his ass with his foot still in it.

McKay bit back curses and spoke quickly, outlining yet another change in plans. Then they moved.

The Guardians had applied camouflage cream to their faces—a dirty-gray base, dabbed with streaks of black, darker gray, brown, white. Even given the rubble-dwellers' propensity for wearing warpaint, wearing obvious camo paint on the move in would have instantly switched the intruders' ID from just another group of armed boffos to men on a mission, exponentially increasing the chance of spooking the game. But at this stage they wanted to break up their silhouettes and reduce the chance of random observation.

McKay and Rogers came out of the laundromat in a hurry, vaulted the low wall where the big corner window used to be, and ran hunkered-over across the street as fast as they could, submachine guns at the ready. They made it without any warning being given.

Once they were among the amorphous heaps of fallen masonry and shattered furniture, the standing walls blocked them from being spotted by anyone in the house—or playing basketball out behind. They had to move carefully, however, to avoid making noise. Out back a noisy dispute broke out over whether a player had carried the ball up-field far enough before driving back in for a shot at the single basket. That helped lots to cover their sound.

They stepped carefully. You never knew in a situation like this whether apparently solid ground wasn't just a bit of cloth or old cardboard covered over with dirt, with a pocket of emptiness below. Such pitfalls occurred frequently in urban ruins, could suck your leg right on down and snap it at the ankle before you could react. But neither McKay nor Rogers was cherry in the rubble, and they moved quickly between the walls that still stood.

"Any action out front?" McKay subvocalized.

"Negative, Billy." Casey replied.

He was up on the second floor of what had once been a reasonably swank apartment building. Like Sloan he was carrying two weapons other than a side arm. He could hardly have lugged his four-foot-long, bull-barreled sniper's rifle along when he might be called on to help in room-clearing. On the other hand, he was a mere seventy-five meters from the building he had to cover, and at that range, with the buttstock of an MP-5 snugged against his shoulder and a half-meter or so sight radius, he could just about drive a nail.

For when he got to close quarters, though, he had slung over his back an Ingram M-10 machine pistol, also in .45 caliber, with a foot-long noise suppressor screwed onto its stub muzzle. It was a vicious little weapon, barely larger than a Colt automatic, with a really vicious cyclic rate and no appreciable accuracy beyond about ten meters. Which made it ideal for the face-to-face combat involved in housecleaning. As a weapon, it made Billy McKay roll up his eyes, almost as much as Sam's nickel-plated Python; but he could see the point of it. Inside of fifty meters Casey's accuracy actually dropped off.

"How's it look on your end?" Casey asked.

McKay and Rogers swapped a look. "Lousy."

The floors were wooden, and might well have been

adequately braced to start with. But much of the bracing was gone, and what remained was anchored to brick walls which themselves were none too steady. They reminded McKay of the smooth plastic building blocks he'd played with as a kid in Pittsburgh. When he and his brothers tired of building houses, sometimes they'd like to poke at the walls to see just how far out of shape they'd go before they came tumbling down. These walls looked just like a chubby infant finger, the size of a Mack truck, had playfully poked them out of true.

McKay had a good eighty pounds on Tom Rogers, so it was obvious who went first. He squatted, linked fingers for a step. The deeply scored rubber sole of one combat boot stepped into it. He straightened and without much effort hoisted the boot up to his breastbone while Rogers grabbed expertly for handholds. Rogers was standing upright on the weathered planking of the second floor.

"How is it? Will it hold my weight?"

"I think so, Billy. But you'd better stay real close to the wall, just in case."

Rogers turned and began scaling a beam that had fallen down from the floor above, agile as a cat. McKay was left to follow as best he could. If the treacherous flooring suddenly decided to worst-case under McKay's two hundred forty pounds, Rogers should be in position to blow the wall and go in anyway.

McKay laid his hand on a two-inch pipe fitting jutting from the wall by his elbow, tested it for solidity. It promptly fell right out of the wall, bringing with it a Frisbee-sized chunk of plaster. McKay just managed to grab it before it all went clattering down into the bricks and boards and shit at his feet.

He peered up. Rogers was already on the fourth

floor, kneeling in the shaft of sunlight and rummaging in his pack. "Fuck *me*," McKay said. He began to climb.

To his astonishment, he found himself hugging the wall at Rogers' side without mishap. Rogers had a black plastic disk a centimeter thick and about the size of a coffee can lid stuck to the wall and was fiddling with it. Red LEDs danced on the back as he calibrated it. This was cutting-edge antiterrorist technology from before the world blew up, a device in whose use the Guardians had trained before the War, and never got a chance to actually play with. Back in the late seventies when a West German team had blown down the doors of a Lufthansa jetliner that had been hijacked to Mogadishu in Somalia, they had known to the square meter where each hijacker would be standing, thanks to the microphones and stethoscopes they had applied to the aircraft's hull.

The device Rogers was using now was a logical development from that, a supersensitive, microcomputer-driven sound sensor that could map an entire room and locate any occupants by the sound of their breathing. A diagram of walls and occupants now appeared on the small screen on its back.

"Two occupants," Tom Rogers said, peering at the little screen and the data flashing to the side. "Both adult males. One by the wall six meters in to the left, the other apparently asleep and right"—he looked up and grinned, tapped the wall six inches above and to the left of the black plastic disk—"here."

He pressed the bell of an old-fashioned stethoscope up against the wall. Like McKay, he had a combat trooper's distrust for fancy Star Wars gimmickry. Nonetheless, most of the special gear the Guardians

were issued worked as advertised. Major Crenna had
seen to that.

A moment passed. Rogers nodded. "Got it," he said,
nodding out of the stethoscope. "The sleeper's there, all
right."

"No sign of the hostages?"

"Black box says they ain't there. We believe it?"

McKay nodded. Rogers pulled what looked like a
flowerpot filled with Silly Putty from his pack and stuck
it on the wall. Then he bent down and reached for
others.

"Company, Billy," Casey said in his ear. "Two bandits. They've come out on the porch."

"No trouble. We're almost ready to—"

The floor gave way beneath McKay's feet.

CHAPTER
TEN ——————————————

McKay's fingernails peeled back as he clawed at the unyielding wall. There was a shocking moment of free fall, then he caught the jagged masonry edge where floor had met wall, held. Broken lumber cascaded into a maelstrom of noise and dust beneath him.

Out on the front stoop of the building, one of the two bandits had just dropped his skinny butt onto the cement slab beside the steps, propped up the wall with his shoulder blades, and lit a cigarette. At the sudden racket he jumped to his feet, hauling at a big pistol stuck through his belt. "What the fuck was that?"

He died. He stood for just a flatfooted moment with his big single-action cowboy pistol in his hand, staring up at the corner of the building. That was all Casey Wilson needed to punch a thumb-sized slug though the flap of his left ear and right through both hemispheres of his brain. He dropped into a rag-doll sprawl.

Billy McKay's boot soles were waving above five or

six meters of dust-choked emptiness. "Blow it, Tom!" he shouted, not bothering to subvocalize.

Another man might have questioned the order, at least paused to check on his comrade and leader. Rogers just stepped to the side and punched the button.

The tiny shaped charges were designed to concentrate a maximum of force and produce a minimum of back-blast, and had been placed with the skill of a demolitions artist. Eye-hurting spikes of incandescent gas stabbed the air and then masonry was collapsing inward in a man-sized hole.

The man sleeping with his back to the west wall was not going to wake up anytime soon; there wasn't a whole lot left of him from the sternum up. His buddy had been sitting on an auditorium chair, playing solitaire, when the wall came tumbling down. He looked up. He just had time to drop his jaw when a figure appeared in the smoke swirling around the sudden hole, and then Rogers shot him twice, the classic antiterrorist double-tap.

The sturdy ex-Green Beret stepped into the room, slid left, glided forward. Behind him a bruised and battered McKay chinned himself up with a single grunting heave, got a boot onto the ledge, and followed, thanking God he'd had to sling his MP-5 to help Rogers pull out explosives. He followed.

Out front, the second bandit stood gaping at the body of his comrade. Then he spun toward the open door, his mouth opening to scream a warning. In a way he was lucky. His move came at the precise instant to throw off Casey's aim, and the bullet intended for his heart caught him high in the left arm, spinning him into the door-jamb.

"It's an attack! I'm hit!" he shrieked. Casey shot him

at the base of the neck, and that was it.

Away across the savaged streets, Casey let a half-held breath out the rest of the way. He hated close-range killings. The war of the skies was so much cleaner, more detached; and you could best your opponent without taking his life. And if you *had* to kill . . . he preferred that there be distance between his will and its consummation. He made himself inhale deeply of air redolent of gunsmoke, hot gun oil, mildew, and dust; blanked his mind, centered himself on void, and was ready.

Hazy Davy pounded down the tarmac with the scavenged ball, driving for the basket though he was barely five-six and the defenders were all over him like a rash. He heard thunder crack all but over his head, paid no attention. He was focused on the goal.

Then he was in position, his wiry legs propelling him into the air, back to the basket, not even looking, and the other team hanging off him, up and up, higher than such a runty little puke should ever jump, half turning, single-handing the ball through the orange hoop so cleanly it never kissed metal.

Perfect.

There was a flashbulb rush of light. Instantly the impromptu court in the niche in back of the building filled up with dense, choking smoke and a million tiny suns thrown out by Sam Sloan's white phosphorous grenade, and the players forgot the game and got down to the serious business of screaming.

Stun grenade in one hand and submachine gun in the other, Tom Rogers dodged out of the room and down the hall. Bleached sunlight spilled in from open doors to his left. An old-fashioned stairwell dropped to his right, along the front of the building. He moved quickly without rushing, totally in control, taking three-second looks into each room as he passed. They were filled with debris, piles of stale bedding and decaying food that gave evidence to his nostrils as well as his eyes of human habitation. But there was no one inside.

Good as he was, Rogers had only two eyes. They were both scoping out the fourth room down when a bandit came boiling out the room at the end of the hall, skidded slightly, and jacked back the bolt of an Uzi.

From the far end of the hall McKay fired a short burst from the shoulder. The bullets caught the man square in the chest and slammed him back against the wall.

Rogers spun past the door he'd been peering in, flashed past another open door to backhand a grenade in the door from which the man had come. Back flattened against the wall for a suspended moment; the awesome flash and noise of the grenade, designed to befuddle enemies for a few crucial seconds. He whirled, snapping his submachine gun up, covering the room. Nothing. He moved back, quickly checked the remaining room. Nothing. He signaled to McKay.

McKay flipped another grenade down the stairwell. It bounced on the first landing below and went off almost in the face of a bandit coming up the stairs to see what the hell was going on. He shrieked, dropped his shotgun, clawed for his eyes with both hands and went tumbling any which way down the stairs.

With a single panther leap, McKay hit the landing. It was a damn-fool stunt, just asking for a busted ankle, but his blood was up. There was no sign of the man he'd grenaded, but right at the foot of the stairs a doorway flew open and a head and a handgun came poking out.

The head glanced up, saw McKay looming above him, jerked back. McKay fired a burst through the door, knocking huge holes in the plywood. In slow motion the man toppled forward and lay still on his face with his blood spilling out over a black plastic runner.

Prepping a stun grenade, McKay pelted downstairs. At their base he tossed it in around the riddled door without even looking. That was the beauty of the things. It didn't matter one damned bit whether the hostages were in the room or not, since the flash-bangs caused no lasting effects. It flashed off with a volcano roar.

He paused—the bandits knew they were being hit by now, and it wasn't unknown for stunned bad guys to have the presence of mind to spray doorways with blind auto-fire in frantic reaction to the detonation. He gave it three, then hopped over the cooling corpse and dived inside, low and left, with Tom covering from the stairs.

The floor was hardwood. The stink was awful. There was nothing in the room but tumbled and incredibly foul bedding, a million candy-bar wrappers, and a bunch of crotch magazines strewn around a piss-and-wine-stained mattress under the window.

Even though time was breathing down his neck like a horny dragon, some instinct made McKay stand up and scope the room out a little further. Ahead and to his right was a little passage obviously leading to a john. His MP-5 ready, he stepped carefully toward it.

And a sliding closet door to his right whipped open and someone sprang out at him, needle-sharp commando dagger upraised in an icepick grip.

McKay ducked and spun, swinging the stubby submachine gun with his right hand. It cracked against the descending elbow. The dagger wheeled past McKay's head and clattered to the floor. He continued his circular motion, grabbing a handful of incredibly dirty T-shirt with his hand and heaving powerfully. Yowling with pain, his attacker went spinning across the room, slammed into a wall, sat down hard.

McKay was over him in a second, pointing the MP-5 at the bridge of his nose. He was hoping he hadn't bent the silencer shroud on the son of a bitch's arm. What he'd caught was an emaciated little specimen who couldn't have been more than seventeen, with a mat of hair that looked as if it had been washed in several colors of tempera paint, but not too recently. He was naked from the waist down, his skinny shanks tattooed with grime. Whether he'd been in there jerking off or was the first man's bun boy, McKay didn't know or care. He was shit-scared, literally, as McKay could tell all too well—and that was just the way McKay wanted him.

The building shook to a low rumble. Sam Sloan was methodically putting the basketball players out of their misery with HE grenades. "Where are the prisoners? The kids you took?"

"D-downstairs. Second floor."

"Which room?"

"Third from the stairs down. No, fourth, fourth. I'm sorry, don't hurt me, I messed up, I—"

McKay silenced him with a boot. He decided it was a legitimate mistake, not a ludicrously misguided attempted to play cagey. "Front of the building?"

The kid only nodded. His lower jaw seemed to be sort of hopping around in his spasms of terror. McKay sub-vocalized a quick message to Rogers. He looked down at the kid, thought about putting one through his skull. *Naw, fuck it. If he gets up the balls to backshoot me, then good for him.* He dashed out into the corridor.

Three doors to his right he heard the muted hammer taps of two silenced shots, a sort of rustling, sliding bump, and silence. He took off down the corridor toward the next flight of stairs, spraying shots into the rooms as he passed—high, just in case the kid was lying or wrong, and avoiding the room from which the shots had come. He wasn't intending to hit anybody, anyway, just keep everybody's head down.

Pausing for a magazine change at the head of the stairs, McKay regretted having a silenced weapon. It didn't make much of an impressive noise, nothing that would keep enemy heads down. Then he remembered something, paused at the head of the stairs, dug a couple of firefight simulators from a pouch on the side of his pack, triggered one and tossed it on the floor. All hell broke loose as he trip-hammered down the stairs— big booms, full-auto rattles, lots of flashes and smoke, the whole nine yards. That would make 'em think twice before poking their noses out.

At the landing he paused to pitch a stun grenade over the railing of the floor below. He could've asked the kid how many of them were there, but he hadn't had the time for light conversation. There were a shitload more than Andy ever told them about, and that was all that mattered.

The corridor filled up with noise as violent as that from upstairs when McKay hit the bottom. He felt a piledriver slam into his left side, staggering him. He sat down heavily at the base of the stairs, held the trigger down, spraying the corridor indiscriminately.

Through the thin blue smoke residue of the stun grenade, McKay could see somebody down at the other end of the corridor blazing away from the hip with some sort of automatic weapon. Plaster dust cascaded over him from the walls and ricochets moaned about like banshees. He flung himself forward on his belly, leading with his own chopper, firing another burst. The shadowy figure stayed on its feet and another muzzle flash reached for McKay.

He lined up the MP-5's thick barrel on the center of

the dark mass and squeezed the trigger. With a scream
the figure staggered backward. McKay held down the
trigger, hosing his enemy, and the tommy gunner went
down, skidded along the floor, and stopped screaming.

McKay rolled onto his right side. The whole left side
of him felt numb. Gingerly he felt himself. The slug had
gouged a long groove in the Kevlar body armor but
hadn't penetrated. It hadn't been a solid hit, thank
God. As it was, he was going to feel awfully sorry when
the shock wore off.

He picked himself up, moved down the hall to the
fourth door on the right. The racket from upstairs was
dying down; he retrieved the second simulator, keyed it,
and tossed it over the railing to give the boys downstairs
something to keep them amused.

The fourth door down was shut. No surprise. McKay
grinned an unpleasant grin. He was going to get to play
Captain Counterterrorist Wonder. He took a couple of
little sticky-fingers charges from a pocket in his coveralls, gave a quick check to the door until he found the
edges of the plates connecting the interior hinges to it.
While the sweet sounds of mock gunfire wafted up from
below, he slapped the little charges in place, activated
the ten-second timers, and stood aside.

The charges cracked off about a second apart. The
door shuddered, then sagged inward. McKay followed it
with a grenade. Three seconds, then he went in too, div-
ing low.

A deafening roar greeted him. Had he been upright
the twin blasts of the sawed-off shotgun would have
caught him from thighs to throat. Instead, a couple of
pellets burrowed into his body armor and the rest
whizzed harmlessly by to blast a huge sheet of yellowing
plaster off the wall above the stairway down.

The smart boy with the shotgun, who'd shut his eyes

when the door blew in, was over by the window hunkered down behind somebody tied to a chair. McKay's flash glance confirmed he had a double-barrel, not an autoloader, which meant he was out of the game for a minute. Over to the left was of all things a huge brass bed. *These assholes know how to do well by themselves,* McKay thought. Naked on the bare mattress, wrists and ankles tied to the dully gleaming uprights, lay a teen-aged girl. She had pretty obviously been raped.

Huddled behind the bed was a bandit with his elbows on the mattress and his hands over his eyes, sobbing. A long black FN lay right up against the girl's leg. That was something about the stun grenades; after having lived through the One-Day War, a lot of people who caught that terrible bright flash made the gut assumption that their eyes were melted, and freaked out totally. McKay shot him between the fingers. Another bad guy had crawled under the bed when the grenade blinded him, which might even had worked had McKay not been lying on his level. A three-round burst took care of him.

McKay turned his attention back to the man huddling behind the captive in the chair. The prisoner was a painfully skinny kid who looked Oriental to McKay. It was only a vague impression, since he looked as if they'd been using him to drive nails. His face was puffed and purple and crusted blood.

The man behind the boy had his shotgun broken open and was trying to stuff two more shells into it but his hands were shaking too badly for him to make much progress. When McKay swung the barrel of the MP-5 his way, he screamed and dropped the gun, then snatched up a butcher knife and held it up against the half-dead Vietnamese kid's neck.

"Go away!" he squawled. "Let me go or I cut him!"

The ugly brown encrustations caked all over the bl

didn't all look like rust, so McKay figured he meant it. Warily he got to his feet.

"Clear out of here without harming the kid and I'll let you go," he said.

The knife jittered, gashing the boy's jaw. He rolled his head and moaned.

"No. Get out! Get out or he dies!" the bandit screamed.

McKay shrugged. "Have it your way."

At his words the knife steadied against the captive boy's throat. Then Tom Rogers, dangling silently outside the window like a giant spider, shot the knife wielder through the back. The knife skidded away across the bare wooden floor. The bandit slumped forward against the back of the chair. His greasy fingers stroked the captive's cheek once, longingly almost, and then he collapsed.

They made it out of the building with only a little more cursory slaughter. It would have been nice to make sure of cleaning out the rest of these scumbags for what they'd done to the kids, but McKay figured it would be best to get the liberated captives to treatment as soon as possible. The girl was bleeding some, and Tom hated to move her as it was. But they had no choice.

Sam Sloan blew in a back door, and he and McKay crossfired the clump of raiders huddled down inside the foyer. The three Guardians left the building half-carrying the semiconscious prisoners. The bodies of three more kidnappers who had tried to make a break for it lay sprawled on the steps and in the street.

"Sorry, Billy," Casey said. "One got away."

"Nobody's perfect."

They hooked back up with their Tide Camp escorts

without incident. "Any trouble?" Tyler asked.

McKay thought about busting his chops on general principles. Instead he just shook his head. "Naw. Piece of cake." The other members of the party improvised stretchers from curtain material and broom handles, and they started home.

After a ways Harris, one of the stretcher-bearers, called to McKay, "Hey, big fella, want to lend a hand?"

McKay gave him a look. The Tide Camp buckos decided to trade off among themselves. They made it back home in time for evening chow.

"The girl has been raped, McKay," Andy Aramyan said.

"No shit." McKay dug a cigar out of a breast pocket.

They were over on the island, with the stretchers laid on the grass next to the Jeff Memorial. The camp's Chinese-American medic and his assistants were tending to the two kids. A couple of orderlies were trying to pry off the Vietnamese boy's mother, who was clinging to his neck and in general carrying on.

"I said you rescue these people, McKay, not let them get all used up first."

McKay studied his cigar and thought about killing the fuck. Sam Sloan must have realized it, because he put a restraining hand on McKay's biceps.

"That's not fair, Aramyan," Sloan said. "We brought them back alive. That's all anybody could ask for."

The Armenian's lip was just curling to shape a reply when one of his boys walked over. "Dink kid's babbling. Says there must have been twenty bad guys at that house." He laughed. "You know how kids exaggerate."

"I'd say that was a fair estimate," Sloan said evenly.

Andy went pale under his soldier of fortune tan. "You don't shit me?"

Sloan shook his head.

The smaller man turned and went over to the stretchers, pushing peremptorily through the attendants. Even the doctor backed off—which was strange to McKay; doctors usually didn't let go of patients until they were good and ready. By this time the girl was conscious and calmer than her boyfriend. Andy spoke to both of them. Then he stood up, looked at the Guardians, and walked quickly off down the island.

Two hours later the Guardians were back in the White House. Having showered the filth and blood off him, and changed into gray Guardians' coveralls—freshly laundered, no less—McKay was getting himself around a hot meal in the private dining room when Soong's assistant Eli Scott showed up.

"I'm terribly sorry," he said. "It was a terrible mistake to send you men into that—that hellhole unsupported. We had no idea how many bandits were there."

"Of course you didn't, Mr. Scott," Tom Rogers said around a mouthful of food. "We know that." His face was, as always, as impassive as a granite block.

Scott made some more comforting noises, then, reassured by the Guardians that all was well, went away again. It had all been a big misunderstanding, but it was cleared up now.

Sure.

By the dawn's early light Andy Aramyan left the warriors' barracks in the memorial for his ritual visit to his own personal crapper, a chemical toilet that looked like a squat plastic model of the defunct Washington Monument. He shut the door, dropped trou, and emplaced himself on the throne.

And a whole cluster of firefight simulators went off about six inches below his hairy rump. The door flew open, and the early-rising occupants of Tide Camp were treated to the spectacle of Andy Aramyan bouncing off over the greensward, hooting and hollering and trailing sparks and smoke and noise like something out of a Warner Brothers cartoon.

Whatever repercussions followed that little incident remained within the confines of the camp. After all, the Guardians were their good friends and allies; they trusted one another. Also, not even the Guardians could sneak in past the constant vigilance of Andy's elite sentries.

Payback was a mother, Billy McKay would have said. But nobody asked him.

CHAPTER
ELEVEN ─────────────

It was another perfect day in the D.C. rubble: hot, humid, and rank as an armpit.

"My mama always tol' me," a Puerto Rican–accented voice said from somewhere in the vast heap of debris, "never talk to no armor cars."

Sitting in the Electronic Systems Officer seat next to Casey, who was at the wheel of Mobile One, Sam Sloan glanced back over his shoulder. "I told you we were going to have to find a more subtle approach."

"So you're right and I'm an asshole," said Billy McKay, leaning over Sloan's shoulder with his jaw clamped on an unlit cigar. Leader or not, the other Guardians would lynch him if he dared light the damned thing. High-tech wonder that it was, there were limits to the capacity of One's life-support system.

"So, like, what'll we do, Billy?" Casey asked, nervously tapping his fingers on the wheel. He wasn't scared; in his own way he was as nerveless as Rogers. It was just that getting behind the wheel acted on him the same way a full moon acted on Lon Chaney, Jr. He wanted to drive real fast and hear loud noises.

"We are going to back off down the street," McKay said, "while Commander Sloan here de-asses the vehicle and talks to these fine people."

Sam swallowed. "You're a pal, McKay."

McKay showed him a shit-eating smirk. "Always." He jerked a thumb toward the top hatch.

The Bloods were sitting around an oil-drum fire, shaking down and cooling off after another hot day. That morning they'd bloodied the noses of a bunch of peckerwood ofay mothers who called themselves the Rebel Runners, who were trying to move in on their scarfin' turf. To celebrate they'd traded for some salvaged wine and batteries at the Rubble Mart, and they had some vintage Aretha on the box and were just in general mellowing down. Most of them used to live in the North Capitol slums hereabouts. Of course it looked different then. This little patch of the night was theirs. In a way, maybe, nothing else had ever been. A lot had burned out after the bombing, but the blast damage hadn't been too bad, and there was plenty of good shelter and even after all this time good scarf. It was no easy life, but not necessarily a bad one.

The fire consisted of weeds carefully dried in derelict buildings, bits of cloth and organic stuff too wretched to reclaim, paper that was beyond reusing. Not good, clean paper, though—that commanded premium barter at the Rubble Mart, God knew why. Some scrap wood, used sparingly. Wood ash and even dust and dirt, packed down and saturated with waste oil. It produced a fitful flame, prone to sparks and hazardous flares. It stank. And the Potomac night didn't call for additional heat. But it provided a focus for warmth of a different sort, and comradeship.

In time the fire burned low. A lot of the brothers and sisters had drifted off to sleep or whatever. The survivors were yawning and stretching and debating whether to call it a night or maybe break out a few jars of bartered homebrew and fuel the party for a while longer. A tall, skinny kid, whose round wire-rimmed spectacles had somehow survived, was just explaining in a high voice how mixing booze like that would give them all ferocious headaches, when somebody noticed there was a stranger sitting at the fire with them.

A moment of rolling eyeballs and hands groping for weapons out of reach. Somebody cursed. Sure, the sentries prowling the boundary of Blood turf resented not being part of the party, but that was no excuse to go slack.

The newcomer didn't move. He just squatted there on his heels, shadowy and silent as one of those funny stone critters they used to put up on top of buildings. A white dude, yeah. But the people were starting to think again now, realizing that if the Rebel Runners were hitting them, they'd have announced their presence with a shower of Molotov cocktails and shotgun blasts, or maybe a grenade in the oil-drum stove. Panic faded, turning to anger—and a bit of curiosity.

"What the fuck you want here, honky?" It was a female voice, hostile and not more than fifteen.

"Just to talk to you." It was a soft voice, with a touch of the Southern that didn't mind anybody to relax. On the other hand, no Rebel Runner had ever talked to a Blood like that, and none ever would. Those bucks had to wear their manhood out in the open for everyone to see.

"Shit," another adolescent voice said. "Le's cut him."

The stranger continued to sit, apparently unaffected by the threats.

"Wait," said the kid with the glasses. "Let's hear what he has to say." He turned to the stranger. "What did you want to talk about?"

"A better life for you, maybe."

A silent moment. The crickets reasserted themselves all around. Nobody'd bothered to turn the tape over the last time it ran out, and the insects reckoned it was their turn.

Somebody laughed, a sound as dry and brittle as unfired pottery. "Shit, man, what we be lackin'? We got our turf, we got plenty of ruins still left to scarf through. Nobody be tellin' us what to do or how to do it. What more we need?"

"We got guns," another voice said darkly.

The newcomer smiled. He wasn't a very big dude, they could see now, but he gave the impression of solidity and strength. "Yeah, you got guns. How would you like not to have to use them so much?"

The Bloods exchanged glances. More of them were coming back out of the darkness, drawn by the earlier commotion. "What, you from the gummint or somethin'? You gonna take over and make things all better for us?"

"I am from the government." Another smile, as if at a private joke. "But I ain't talking about taking anything away from you. Especially not your freedom. You can keep on building a life for yourself like you've been. But maybe we can offer you a chance to get an even better return on your efforts. And not have to spend so much blood to stay alive."

"Shit. We can take care of ourselves. We be bad."
An adolescent voice, crackling with high-tension bravado.

"Hold on," said the kid with the glasses. He for one wasn't forgetting the Rebs were a long way from out of it. Or the Warlords, or the Pagans, or the Death Commandos, and the dozens of other gangs scrabbling in the ruins of Washington, D.C. "There was eighty-five of us when we moved back into the city last summer. Now there's forty. It might just be we're interested, Mister, but what do you want from us?"

"Alliance."

Skeptical looks circled the fire. "What gang you run with? You too good a dresser to be a runner." He meant a member of an adult urban gang, of which the Rebel Runners were just one bad example.

"Who's your main man?" asked another.

"I'm with the Guardians," the stranger said. "Our main man is Jeffrey MacGregor. The President of the United States."

"Well, looky here," said the skinny white kid with the brush haircut, denim vest, and white T-shirt. "Live meat."

The half-dozen adolescent boys and girls stared with contemptuous surprise at the man standing out in front of the former office building that was the Warlords' clubhouse.

A burly blond youth stepped out of the darkened entryway to join them on the cement steps. He took a slip from a bottle of scarfed Tuborg.

"Welcome to Warlords' turf," he said. "Got anything to say before you're too busy screaming?"

The stranger didn't even bat an eye. He was tall and looked pretty trim for an old man who had to be crowding thirty-five. He had brown hair and an oblong country face and lopsided smile that, molasses like, began to appear. "There are one or two things I'd like to discuss with you."

" 'There are one or two things I'd like to discuss with you,' " a girl mimicked through her upturned nose. She was wearing a grubby white blouse, faded pink stretch pants, magenta batwing shades.

Late fifties nostalgia is surely hard on the eyes, Sam Sloan thought.

"Why don't you take him down, Billy? Maybe he's got some good dope on him," another kid suggested.

The big blond youth sipped his beer, nodded briskly at Sloan. A couple of the loungers unfolded themselves from the steps and started toward him.

"Hold it." The words weren't shouted, but something in their tone brought the two up short. The stranger seemed to have grown an inch or two taller, and there was a look in his eyes that made them distinctly uncomfortable. "You there. Big boy. What I'd like you to do is hold that beer bottle up over your head."

They looked at him. The blond kid lowered his jaw to his neck and stared at Sloan as if unsure whether to kill him on the spot or humor him.

"Don't do it, Billy," squealed a girl with hair like black straw. "It's a trick."

That settled it. He was the warlord of the Warlords in the middle of his own turf, and if anybody was dumb enough to call him, he sure wasn't going to back down. Slowly he began to raise the bottle.

"That's it," Sloan said approvingly. "Real high now. Hold it just by the fingertips."

"Okay," Billy said. "What happens now?"

The bottle exploded.

A male voice screamed. Kids started to go in all directions like fragments of an exploding grenade.

"Not so fast," the stranger said in that whipcrack voice. Once again it held them.

Billy was standing up there with his arm upraised like the Statue of Liberty, his head and shoulders dusted with beer bottle fragments like angular amber snow. He blinked dumbly down at Sloan.

"As I said, there are some things I'd like to discuss with you," Sloan continued, silently thankful that Casey's aim wasn't off today. "Now, we can discuss things in a nice, mature manner. Or—"

He turned and gestured up the street. As he did so a pounding roar thundered briefly, seemingly from all around, and the facade of a three-story building exploded in gouts of bricks and dust and smoke three blocks away.

"—or we will have to take some very stern measures." The entire front of the building slumped into ruin.

"Precisely what is it you gentlemen have in mind?" asked the shaven-headed black man with silver in his full, neatly trimmed beard.

That son of a bitch is big, McKay thought.

He, Sam, and Tom were sitting around an antique-looking table in the echoing emptiness of the sitting-room or parlor—or maybe it was a ballroom, who the hell knew?—of what had been an elegant house between Sixteenth Street and Rock Creek Park, up north almost to the Maryland line. Morning sunlight spilled across a polished hardwood floor from an open door. Through it also came voices, footsteps, small thumps and scrapes, the generic sounds of work. Casey Wilson was out keeping an eye on Mobile One. This was not considered a high-risk area.

Hell, it wouldn't surprise me if these folks were a damn sight more reliable than Soong's gang of wackos, McKay ruminated.

He sat back, half tuned-out as Sam and Tom pitched the many benefits of alliance to their host. The host was quite a specimen. He was a good two meters tall, with a high forehead that gleamed like burnished mahogany. He carried himself and spoke with the dignity and erudition McKay (who'd never been within a light-year of the Ivy League) imagined would suit a professor at a prestigious Ivy League college. Which he had been. Somehow his speech and bearing didn't go oddly with the khaki workshirt and sun-faded dungarees and huge, scarred, steel-tipped boots he wore, or the calluses on his dinner-plate hands. Even the little round wire-rimmed spectacles he wore perched on his nose, which would have looked utterly ridiculous on someone smaller or with a whit less dignity, looked somehow right. The dude was *impressive.*

Not all of the factions crawling through the rubble were kid gangs. Some of them weren't gangs at all. Tide Camp was one, of course, though McKay had his definite doubts about Andy's little friends. These people comprised another. They were more settlers than anything else. They seemed to have no particular name for themselves, though they were commonly known as "Gold Coasters," after the formerly affluent black neighborhood in which they'd staked out their territory, moving back into the city after the fallout died back. It was a community of a couple of hundred people ranging from former residents of this area to ghetto kids little different from the Bloods Tom Rogers had sweet-talked into the fold a few nights before. Aside from the fact they were almost all black, they had nothing in common McKay could see beyond the personality of this man.

At the moment the Gold Coast's guru was listening to the pitch in grave silence, a slight frown slowly engraving itself between his brows. The conversation was beginning to bog. Rogers was more used to dealing with wild-eyed natives running through the bush waving Kalashnikovs over their heads than former Princeton professors. Sloan, something of an intellectual himself, was impressed with the man's credentials, as well as possessing the usual white liberal tendency to slip off-center in the presence of ethnics. Consequently Tom had clammed up and Sloan was starting to run at the mouth. McKay was about to intervene when their host, with exquisite timing, gave Sam the coup de grace when he paused to draw breath.

"It seems to me that what you're saying, Commander Sloan, is that speaking on behalf of the Government of the United States, such as it is, you are willing to extend your benevolent influence over our community. I'm not altogether sure we want that."

Sam opened his mouth, shut it, swallowed. "Oh, really?"

McKay rolled his eyes. *Oh Christ, not another one.*

"Not another economist," he'd howled during the morning's briefing by Eli Scott at the White House. "Why does it have to be economists? We always find economists."

"That's because we were sent out to look for them, Billy," Casey said. "They're an important part of the Blueprint for Renewal."

"Yeah. But so are computer scientists, and we don't always find computer scientists. And we don't always find civil engineers, and we don't always find astrophysicists, and we don't always find psychologists. What we always find are economists."

"Oh, but Dr. McDaniels isn't just an economist," Scott put in soothingly. "He's also a lawyer, historian, and a political analyst. His theories are rather unorthodox, but he is truly an impressive figure."

And McKay was truly impressed with Dr. Josephus McDaniels, but not for the same reasons. He was mainly impressed because the dude looked like he could tie McKay up in a knot and roll him down the street with a stick, like a kid with a tire. You didn't see many economists with shoulders like that.

"The people of this community are only too aware of how the benevolent attentions of the government kept the majority of them—most blacks—subservient and stagnant by rendering the dependence more profitable than enterprise. That's one point on which we agree with my esteemed colleague, Mr. Jabbar, as well as the more orthodox Black Muslims," Dr. McDaniels was saying now.

"Jabbar?" McKay asked.

McDaniels looked startled. "Malcolm Jabbar, head of the New American Nation of Islam, Inc., another pre-War figure come back to haunt the capital, like me and Mr. Rushton of the Union."

"Madden mentioned him to us, McKay," Sloan said. "He's got a following down in Anacostia, across the river."

"But I digress. We are making strides toward a self-sufficiency here, in the midst of devastation—through scavenging, through trade, through cultivation—"

"I notice your people have cleared a good stretch of the park for cultivation," Sloan said. "I have to admit it puts me off a bit, to see the park torn up like that."

"Would you prefer that these people should starve,

like tribesfolk rotting in shantytowns on the borders of the ancestral lands from which they were driven to create game preserves? I do not believe that survival is optional, Commander Sloan.''

McKay perked up. At first he'd thought McDaniels was a crank of the same bent as the anarchists of Colorado's Freehold. Now he'd said something McKay could get a grip on.

"That's exactly what we're talking about, Dr. McDaniels," he began, linking his fingers and leaning forward to thump them on the polished tabletop before him. He ignored a heavenward rolling of eyes by Sloan, who was under the impression his fearless leader couldn't open his mouth in polite company without trying to take a bite out of his boondockers.

"I think that's what we're talking about here," he continued. "Survival. On our side, survival for the President. And not just for him, but maybe for the future of this country, if it's even gonna have a future. And for you, too. We're talking about cleaning up the rubble, putting the blocks to all these raids and warfare and shi—stuff. You can't tell me that won't benefit your people, Doctor."

He leaned back, feeling oddly drained, convinced he'd made a jerk out of himself.

"Bravo," Sloan subvocalized over the commnet. McKay couldn't tell whether he meant it or not; he had that damned hillbilly poker face on.

McDaniels stared out the unglazed window into the juniper bush outside, drumming his big blunt fingers on the tabletop. "There is much in what you say, Lieutenant McKay," he said at last, turning back to the table. "Tell me more."

•   •   •

"Welcome, gentlemen, to the epicenter of the New America." The blond man swept his arm in an all-encompassing circle as his words skittered up to the top of the Rotunda dome almost sixty meters overhead. "Starting from here, we're going to build a new era of economic democracy for this country—with all due respect to your President MacGregor, of course."

"Keep cool," Sloan subvocalized to McKay, whose already thick neck was beginning to swell and turn an interesting shade of red.

"I'm forgetting my manners," the blond guy said, stepping forward with hand extended. He was about medium height, with shaggy hair, a handlebar mustache, blue eyes seeming to drift around behind the windows of thick glasses with square steel rims. He was wearing blue jeans and workboots and a blue chambray shirt with what looked like some sort of Aztec designs embroidered on it in rust and ocher. The style of his hair and mustache made him look to Sloan like someone who was trying to hang on to thirty a little longer than was graceful. The hand he proffered showed no calluses. "I'm Seth Rushton, head of the American Union. I'm, ah, pleased to meet you."

Sloan took his hand. "A pleasure. I'm Samuel Sloan. This is William McKay, head of the Guardians."

"Uh." McKay took Rushton's hand, caught Sloan giving him the fish eye, let it go instead of crushing it to pulp.

That was as far as the introductions went on their side. Tom and Casey were parked outside in the car; this was Indian country or damn near to it, even though it was in rock-throwing distance of the Guardians' base of operations. Sloan wondered wryly if Casey had been hanging out with his anarchist lady friend Angie enough to actively enjoy busting down the doors of the United States Capitol with a ten-ton armored car if he had to come to rescue his buddies.

Like the White House itself, the Capitol had not sustained much serious damage from the bombing, miraculously enough. What cosmetic damage had been done had mostly been cleaned up by Rushton's busy AU gnomes, with the exception of the Statue of Freedom, which used to stand up on top of the whole structure. She lay half embedded on her right side in the floor of the Rotunda, not looking altogether comfortable. She was six meters long and heavy enough to bust through the cast-iron dome when the bomb blasts pushed her off her perch, so she would not have been convenient to relocate.

Rushton recovered his hand from McKay as if wishing he could tactfully wipe it on his jeans. "This is Marcie FitzAllan, an esteemed political associate, and also my wife." He quirked up the corners of his mustache at this, as if it were a joke of some sort.

Marcie stepped forward, a woman of about her husband's age and an inch or so shy of his height, with straight blond hair and an embroidered white blouse. For all his determination to be free of male chauvinism, Sam couldn't help noticing that she was more than a handsome woman, slender, if a bit drawn in the features. She reminded him of Susan Spinelli, Assistant Director of the Blueprint-linked New Eden commune and agricultural research facility in the Sierra Nevada of California, with whom he'd had an all-too-brief affair the year before—and who was now almost certainly a prisoner of the FSE Expeditionary Force. Not that she looked like Susan, really, but that hair, so straight and blond and long . . .

Her grip was strong and dry, her voice cordial and

well modulated, though he'd been too lost in his own head to hear what she said. McKay took her hand a lot more readily than he'd taken her husband's. Sloan stepped on the urge to sigh. Present McKay with a female of even moderate attractiveness and it was hungry-like-the-wolf time.

"Last but not least—no, no, a long way from it—I would like to present to you a colleague, a comrade if you will, who is also going to be a major factor in the rebuilding of America. Mr. Malcolm Jabbar."

The final member of the little knot of people standing in the middle of the ringing emptiness of the Rotunda stepped forward. He was wearing a dark blue three-piece suit with an indigo tie, and looked as if he'd just stepped over from the Federal Courthouse after cementing some schmuck of a trafficker into Fort Leavenworth. He was very small and very dark and very, very hard. His features looked as if they'd been carved out of obsidian like an Aztec idol. His grip on Sloan's hand was like a robot claw, as cool and unyielding as steel. He said nothing, just tipped his head forward a few inches then turned to McKay.

McKay's paw enfolded Jabbar's hand like a catcher's mitt, but he wasn't playing any knucklebusting games. After all this time, Sloan could practically read his leader's mind. McKay was wondering what Marcie Fitz-Allan was like in the sack. He was wondering, not so much what an obvious goofball like Seth Rushton was doing in charge of a faction that held claim to some of the heaviest-duty turf in the rubble, but what he was doing still breathing.

But about Malcolm Jabbar McKay wasn't wondering one bit. With the instincts of a Pittsburgh street kid, a Beirut street fighter, a Studies and Observations Group dirty-warfare specialist who'd fought all over the southern and eastern Med, he had instantly sized Jabbar up as a man always to be watched, an operator, a man who knew moves. A stone killer.

What he was doing with the likes of Seth Rushton was, Sam thought, a very good question.

"We have a proposition for you," Sam began.

"We would be more than happy to meet with the President," Rushton said cheerfully. "It's high time steps were taken to reinstitute proper democratic procedures, so that the people can make their will known and we can begin to institute real economic justice in this country."

While McKay and Sloan goggled at him, he plowed inexorably onward. "In the meantime we have demands which are, you might say, non-negotiable. First and foremost among these, of course, is that you surrender to us the Bureau of Engraving and Printing."

"What the fu—" Sloan brought McKay up short with a quick heel to the instep.

"We feel that it is vital to resume printing money as soon as possible, reopening the floodgates of wealth, which will sweep this country to real prosperity. Production of money is vital to stimulating the economy, so that it can once again begin to provide consumer merchandise to the people—not that they really need it, you understand, but at first it will help build morale, and through proper vigilance we can ensure that the means of production do not pass into the hands of exploiters, while insuring a steady stream of consumer goods—"

A loud buzzing had begun in Sloan's ears. He wasn't sure whether to try to shove a word in edgewise or just bust up laughing. McKay looked as if he just wanted to pick Rushton up and shake him. Sloan wasn't sure he'd try to stop him if he did. Through the whole diatribe Marcie and Jabbar stood well away from Rushton,

Marcie looking pained, Jabbar cool and impermeable as volcanic glass.

"Mr. Rushton, you'll have to excuse me," Sam finally said, holding up his hands, fighting to keep a straight face. "All these are policy matters which we, frankly, are not competent to discuss. We're merely, uh—"

"Grunts," McKay supplied.

Shooting him a venomous sidelong look, Sloan said, "Soldiers, merely trying to open channels of communication on behalf of the President of the United States. You will have to take these matters up with President MacGregor—and, ah, Mr. Soong, whom I believe actually controls the Bureau."

Rushton frowned, blinked rapidly. "I suppose. What *are* you competent to talk about?"

"We're attempting to draw together as many of the factions here in the capital as possible. This will work to everyone's benefit, by . . ."

"These are some nutty fuckers," McKay remarked as they walked down the broad steps of the Capitol.

"Indeed. But at least we've got them talking. And when they're doing that they're not jumping us." Sloan laughed. "Somehow, I don't think it'll take a whole hell of a lot to keep Rushton talking till the end of time."

When the two Guardians had left through the vast bronze doors that had Christopher Columbus chiseled all over them, a man stepped out of the darkness of a side passage.

Rushton turned toward him eagerly. "They did just what you said they would, Ian. They want to open talks. And they don't suspect a thing. How did I do? I did well, didn't I?"

"Yes, Seth. Very well. A trifle ebullient, perhaps, but well." Colonel Ivan Vesensky, late of the KGB, took a small foil packet from the pocket of his shirt, unfolded one end, shook a few grams of his personally blended granola into his palm, munched it. "I think things are going just as we wish them to."

CHAPTER

TWELVE ——————————

"Mayday! Mayday!" Heads turned in Mobile One as Casey cranked the volume of the radio monitor up high. "This is Tide Team Bravo Three, inbound on forager-escort duty. We've hit a roadblock and are under attack. Please assist immediately." In the background could be heard the steady hardwood knocking of one of the big FNs the Tidal warriors favored. The voice rapped off a map reference while somebody screamed in the background.

"Where the fuck is that?" demanded McKay, who had the wheel. It was just after sunset and the Guardians were inbound themselves, back from a little hearts-and-minds work among a group that called itself the Super Machos.

Sloan had a map grid-marked for them by the Tide Camp people, squinting at it in the glow of an overhead light. "I've got it, Billy."

"Talk me in." McKay punched a button on the communications console. "Bravo Three, this is Guardians. We're on our way."

Static sizzled on the radio. "—careful. Attackers have antitank—" The signal fuzzed out again.

"Great," Sloan said.

"The bastards are getting bold," McKay said.

"Maybe we're rattling some cages," Rogers said from the rear of the vehicle.

This was the third ambush of Tide Camp personnel in four days, and they had five men killed and six injured already. It looked as if some of the wilder and woolier elements in the rubble, fearing their style would be cramped by the proposed alliance, were trying to pinch it off before it had a chance to grow.

McKay brought the big car bucketing to a stop. "They're about a klick from here. Case, shag your ass down here and take over. Sam, you're in the turret." He swivelled the driver's seat and stood, hunched over in the confines of the car. "We need to make some time."

The Tide Camp convoy was jammed up in an urban renewal area north of New York Avenue, where the process of razing poor folks' homes to make room for the bourgeois bureaucracy had been rudely interrupted by the One-Day War. Only a madman would have tried to negotiate the rubble-choked streets at high speed, after dark, with lights out. Only an inspired madman would have had a chance of success. Which was why McKay called on Casey Wilson to drive.

The V-450 took off as if it had afterburners. Moving into the ESO seat, McKay fastened his seatbelt tightly to avoid bouncing the top of his crewcut head off the overhead deck, closed his eyes, ignored the way his kidneys were getting jounced loose from their moorings, and tried to concentrate on nice, soothing pastimes such as ambush-busting.

It was a relatively uneventful journey, considering who was at the wheel. They smashed only three derelict cars, drove through only one brick wall (which was no longer up to code, anyway), plowed through only one mound of debris that must have come up to McKay's breastbone, and knocked the front end off of only one burned-out Metrobus before they were in position.

McKay popped the front top hatch and poked his head out into the muggy evening. The sound of the firefight going on a few blocks away hit him like a slap. He hoisted himself out, crouched on the deck surveying the smears of oxidized paint, pulverized brick dust, oil and dirt and bits of rags and unidentifiable stuff smeared all over Mobile One's sharply angled bow.

"Jesus," he subvocalized. "I hope our insurance is paid up on this thing." He dropped to the street next to the car.

Noiseless as a shadow Rogers joined him as he checked to make sure his Aussie box was firmly clamped to the side of his M-60. There was going to be no dicking around with silenced submachine guns and hostage-rescue drill. This time they were going in to kick asses and take names. With a muted dyspeptic grumbling of its diesel, Mobile One backed up and disappeared down a side street as Rogers and McKay split to different sides of this avenue and became one with the night.

It was a classic ambush. The Tide Camp convoy consisted of a couple of pickup trucks, a big Toyota four-wheeler, and an armored car jerry-rigged out of metal plates and sandbags leading off. The ambushers had waited until it headed down a street whose buildings had suffered little gross blast damage. As the lead car neared the end of the block a panel truck had suddenly popped out of a side street and halted, blocking the road. At the same instant a well-placed demo charge had dropped the front of a building behind the last vehicle, cutting off escape.

Even as the Tide Camp gunner in the lead car's improvised mount had swung his M-249 machine gun to spray the blocking truck a Light Antitank Weapon— LAW—had struck his side of the vehicle, blowing mount and gunner into lasagna and half-cooking the driver. For the convoy it was a very sticky situation.

For the Guardians, who had been driven from pillar to post by the overwhelmingly superior might of the Effsees, and who were beginning to feel the strains of dealing with Andy Aramyan and his boys, it was pure R & R.

Six or eight attackers were hiding behind the panel truck and makeshift barricades at the head of the block. Others were firing down on the hapless victims from the upper stories of the buildings to either side of the street, their high angle meaning they didn't have to worry about crossfiring one another, as well as making it hard for the defenders to hide.

As he went down on his belly not forty meters behind the blocking force, McKay was surprised to see the street splashed with the yellow glares of what had to be Molotov cocktails. *Looks like they're more interested in destroying the convoy than looting it.* As mysteries went, it didn't bug him much. Part of Tom Rogers's assignment was to get them some answers about the recent attacks.

"I'm set, Billy," came Rogers's voice.

"Case?"

"Roger, Billy. We're all set."

McKay slipped his finger inside the trigger guard, dropped his left hand onto the black metal buttstock of the machine gun and brought it up tight against his shoulder. "Rock and roll."

At his first burst a burly ambusher firing an M-16 across the hood of the panel truck came apart like a can of Pillsbury rolls. Crouching by the bumper, a second swirled, trying to bring up an Uzi—every precinct house and federal agency arsenal in the District was full of the damned things—and the stubby SMG went flying up in the air as the ambusher rolled screaming into the open. McKay was pumping the trigger, squeezing short bursts so rapidly they were almost one long one, letting the weapon's natural muzzle jump spray the ambushers with lead.

Muzzle flashes still flickered like fireflies on speed from third stories on both sides of the street. Suddenly the building fronts to the east lit up like an old-time movie marquee. Chunks of masonry avalanched into the street. Even above the gunfire, screams could be heard as white phosphorus grenades interspersed with the HEDP rounds Sloan had slammed into the building kicked in.

The blocking force split to both sides of the street. McKay smiled and swung the muzzle of his machine gun to the right. This was going to be the lucky day for one of the guys who'd gone left. The others . . . he opened fire, swinging the stream of bullets like a scythe.

Crouched down behind a busted-out picture window, Tom Rogers thought two of the fleeing ambushers were heading straight for him. That could have gotten a bit complicated, but even as he thought it the first one ducked into the next door down from the little stationery shop.

Amidst the yammer of McKay's MG and the dancing-giant pounding of the .50 caliber in Mobile One's turret as Sloan worked over the eastern side of the street, Rogers could barely hear the pop of his own 5.56 Galil. The slower ambusher dropped kicking to the sidewalk next to the door the first had gone into. Rogers fired a careful shot into the man's head, then flowed over the low sill like carbon dioxide smoke.

There were no heroes among the ambushers—at least none who made it through the Guardians' initial onslaught. Whoever survived the inferno Sloan made of the upper floors of the buildings on the eastern side of the street got the message right away. So did the team on the other side. They were basically untouched, but they knew when they were decisively outpointed, and did a fast fade. Billy McKay spattered some rounds into the building they'd occupied, to make sure, but no more fire came from that direction. The whole thing was over in less than a minute.

As McKay packed up his MG and walked down the street to see what kind of assistance the battered Tide Camp troopies needed, Rogers gave him a call. "Got a prisoner, Billy." He emerged from a building to the left as Mobile One came rolling up in front of the blocking truck, toting a figure in a fireman's carry.

"Stick him in the car and let Case secure him while Sloan covers. Then give me a hand with the convoy." Rogers nodded and walked over to the vehicle, carrying his burden without apparent effort.

The convoy had been very lucky. There was nothing to be done for the armored car's gunner, and the driver had been badly burned by the same missile. The team commander had been riding up front next to the driver. He was fairly comprehensively scorched and punctured in various places, but refused treatment. Three people in the other vehicles had been hit, and a fourth had taken a round through the head. He was still breathing, but gave that up when Rogers was examining him.

Tom did what he could for the wounded, then climbed back into Mobile One to take charge of the prisoner while Casey bulldozed the panel truck out of the way, which he did with more gusto than McKay thought necessary. McKay hooked the big Cadillac Gage's tow cable to the damaged armored car and climbed back into Mobile One.

"How's the prisoner coming?" he asked, turning to slip his machine gun into the padded clamps that held it against the hull.

"Think she's coming around," Tom Rogers said.

It took a moment to sink in. "Say what?"

The vehicle started moving, the engine racing slightly as the tow line tautened, then evening out as the vehicle moved off. McKay looked toward the back of the car, where Tom was sitting on a fold-down seat. Next to him sat the prisoner, arms secured behind her back by special nylon restraining wraps, shackled to a tiedown in the deck. The person was small and shapeless in an army jacket and cammie pants, the hair was cut short, but the fine dark features were clearly feminine. As McKay stood and stared the eyes opened, startling white slits of hatred glaring up at him.

"Glad you could join us, sister," he said. "What's the name and what's the game?"

She shook her head, elevated it on her slender neck. "I am Marshal Commander Uhuru Assad of the Cinque Battalion of the Black Liberation Army. I consider myself to be a prisoner of war. I refuse to answer any more questions."

"Well I," Billy McKay said, "will be dipped in shit."

Ivan Vesensky was beyond question the finest all-around operative in the vast Soviet apparatus, which was why Yevgeny Maximov had taken such exquisite pains to convince him to turn his coat. What he loved most of all, the work at which he considered himself an unmatched *artiste*, was that of control and cadre. Manipulating agents and allies in foreign lands in the interests of, first, the Soviets, and subsequently Maximov.

He had felt himself wasted as political advisor to FSE military government in California. Not that General Maitland was not providing a valuable service. General Maitland was a sufficiently good military man—which meant, in Vesensky's judgment, sufficiently stolid and unimaginative that he would not on his own create a fiasco, as someone with more initiative might. On the other hand, his notion of how to run an ant farm was to pull out the ants and stomp on them if they didn't build tunnels he liked. Not that that approach was unfamiliar to Vesensky; it was pure Soviet Army, which was a big reason he'd gone into the KGB instead of the military. So it was good for Chairman Maximov's grand scheme that Vesensky was on hand to keep the military government's clubfootedness from rendering its subjects totally intractable. Nevertheless, it was hitching a fine steeplechaser to a plow—Vesensky loved metaphors.

To coin another one, the people Vesensky manipulated shared a lot of characteristics with fulminate of mercury. They might go off at any time. They were the fringe elements in a society, the zealots and zanies of the right as well as left. By playing to their fantasies and fanaticisms, Vesensky was able to work them like a demo specialist working moldable plastic explosives. And, like an explosives expert, he knew there was always the chance they'd go off in his face. That had almost happened to him in California, where longtime Soviet sleeper and former Lieutenant Governor Geoffrey van Damm had finally detonated in a paroxysm of megalomania, trying at the last to purge even his old friend and control "Ian Victor"—Vesensky's cover name. Vesensky was only just able to escape with his life—taking with him most of the explosives intended to trigger the recovered thermonuclear device van Damm imagined to be his ace in the hole.

He was working with substances just as volatile here. For one thing, he didn't have a wide assortment of Soviet-infiltrated nut groups to work with, the way he had in California; the Washington network, from agitators and terrorists to the pasty-faced bureaucrats of the KGB *Residenz* in the Embassy, had been pretty much eradicated by the fallout blanket that smothered the city after the bombing. Like the Guardians, he found himself having to deal with street gangs of unknown allegiance and predictable unreliability.

But he was not without resources. Seth Rushton was one. He was no Stalinist, no self-acknowledged traitor, as van Damm had been. He basically bought the notion that Soviet society worked the way it was supposed to on paper, was indeed a workers' paradise. His vision of rebuilding America was a sort of populist Sovietization.

He was not as much of an idiot as he had come off in the interview with the Guardians—dealing with enemies, two members of an ultra-elite team, all the while keeping a secret, brought out the worst James Bond instincts in him. He was in fact an organizer and a manager of genius, which was why he'd been able to take a following back into the ruins with him, and why they'd made it this long. He was, of course, insane, and tended to get obsessive about his cargo cult dream of restoring the flow of consumer goods. But that was fine with Vesensky; it gave him a splendid handle.

Then there was Jabbar. Jabbar was no communist. He was, in fact, an all but upfront fascist, and his proclivity for making inflammatory statements about Jews had driven the American media to commit the heresy of criticizing a black leader, even comparing him to Hitler.

But the USSR had never really minded fascists very much, except for an unfortunate misunderstanding with Hitler, and since World War II the Soviets had been generally willing to provide arms, advice, and training to fascist terrorists on the same terms as they did to leftists: that they paid premium prices.

Malcolm Jabbar had knowingly dealt with Soviet agents in the past, and moreover had strong ties to openly revolutionary groups, such as the Black Liberation Army, to whom he was publicly hostile, and who had a presence of their own in the rubble. He and Vesensky could deal. And because he was not mad—at least not if you excluded his ethnic and economic theories—he was more able than Rushton.

He was commensurately harder to control.

To his two human detonators, Rushton and Jabbar, Vesensky was adding the nitroglycerine of the real outlaw gangs. McKay had guessed right about that; the alliance the Guardians were trying to cobble together was cramping the style of the real badass bands. Vesensky was working that angle too.

He enjoyed this. The Guardians were the worthiest foes he'd ever encountered. They had gotten the best of him in California. Now they were almost precisely where he wanted them.

And best of all, they were putting themselves there.

CHAPTER
THIRTEEN ——————————

"Let's take it again, nice and slow," Billy McKay said, massaging the bruise on his cheekbone. "Why were you attacking the convoy?"

The prisoner glowered up at them with her cheek pressed to the thin puce carpet of the downstairs cubicle. Her arms were bound behind her to the back of a swivel chair that now lay on its side on the floor.

"Let me up, you fascist cocksuckers." Her nostrils were flared wide, her chest was pumping like a bellows with anger and the exertion that had toppled her seconds before.

The four Guardians ignored her outburst. *She ain't too bad looking,* McKay thought. He noticed things like that, even in the weirdest circumstances. Her features were chiseled and fine, and when he'd helped escort her out of Mobile One he'd ascertained in passing that she had all the right curves in all the right places, not voluptuous, but trim and hard. Of course, right about then, she'd butted him in the face and kicked Sam Sloan with both feet, knocking the wind out of him, and he'd had to slug her to subdue her. Still, she was pretty fine looking.

She reeled in a quavery breath. "I'm Uhuru Assad of the Black Liberation Army," she moaned. She began thrusting sideways at the carpet with her legs, seemingly trying to right herself by force of will. "I am a prisoner of war. Let me up, you honky bastards!"

"Why'd you jump the convoy?" Tom asked quietly.

In response she managed to twist her wiry body to get both feet on the floor, heaved mightily. The chair clanked erect, teetered for a second, then pitched over in the other direction with a clatter and a massive thud, followed by a smaller, softer echo as her head thumped the floor. Sam winced. She reminded him of a wild animal in a trap.

"Shouldn't we better do something before she hurts herself?" he subvocalized.

"Negative," Rogers returned. "Let her work it off."

"The convoy," he said.

"We were striking a blow against those who are trying to restore the fascist Amerika to prey upon the lives of the people," she said in a low, throbbing voice. She lay still for the moment.

"Who else is involved in these attacks?" Sloan asked. "Yours isn't the only group."

"The people are spontaneously arising against the oppressor. *Let me go!*" She began to thrash like a beached fish, rattling the heavy chair.

"Let's let her think about it for a while," Rogers said.

McKay frowned at him a moment, then walked over, keeping out of range of her flying feet—they'd deprived her of her combat boots when they'd frisked her earlier—and picked up the chair and set it on its base. "We're gonna leave you alone now. You got water and even a john that works." Soong insisted on having his people haul tankloads of fresh water, distilled from the Potomac, to the White House each day. It seemed very important to him that the President of the United States not have to crap in a chemical toilet. "We're even gonna feed you. See how nice we are?"

She snapped her head around, tried to spit at him, missed. He hunkered down and caught her in a full Nelson, arms pinned, his fingers interlaced behind her neck, while Tom released the bonds that held her to the chair. McKay straightened, holding her effortlessly off the floor. The other Guardians left the room. McKay carried her to the door, turned, pushed her away. She went in a heap. He quickly stepped out and closed the door.

Outside, Sloan and Casey were looking visibly relieved.

"I thought you were going to, like, interrogate her," Casey said. He wasn't referring to the relatively mild questioning. Guardians training had included exposure to a wide variety of interrogation techniques, both from the questioner's and, in carefully controlled circumstances, the victim's role. It had not been either man's favorite part of the program.

"Maybe later," McKay rumbled, and walked off down the hall.

"Marcie."

"Huh?" She pried an eye open. She could feel the heat of his skinny body behind her, propped up on an elbow. He couldn't sleep and wanted to talk. Again. She sighed, rolled over onto her back.

Now he was poised with his elbow digging into the

salvaged mattress and his cheek braced on his palm. He was going to make her ask. "What is it?"

"It's those Guardians. Such . . . militarists." He shivered. "They could cause us trouble."

"Your friend Ian says different." She couldn't read that one. He was a fox, with those sea green eyes and blond sun-bleached hair, his ski instructor's build, his hint of British public school accent. And he seemed sexless, somehow. She had tried a few come-ons, nothing serious. Nothing. He was unresponsive. And oh, so mysterious.

Irritated, Seth shook his head with a wet-spaniel motion. "Something's happened. Jabbar's right-hand woman has been captured. Uhuru Assad."

"I thought she was his squeeze. I thought it was gauche, anyway, how she combined Swahili and Arabic names like that."

"But don't you see? What if they make her talk?"

"She'll never break. She's ghetto-bred, tough." *Not like some people I know,* she bit off in time.

"But I'm sure they're thoroughly indoctrinated in CIA interrogation techniques! They can make anybody talk."

She sighed again, hiked herself to a sitting position. The air was still, lifeless. She wished again that they could run the ventilation at night, but fuel for the emergency generators was rare, even though the things weren't picky, and the Union didn't have anyone who could maintain them. "She's a dedicated revolutionary. Quit being so melodramatic."

"You're right." He lay back on the mattress.

But in a moment he was snuggling up against the taut curve of her hip. She sighed and rolled onto her back. He hadn't cooled down. His rigid little dick poked into the curve of her thigh, hot as a firebrand. One way or another he wasn't going to let her sleep.

The only thing left was to distract him. She let her fingers travel down to the lower hem of the overlong T-shirt he always wore to bed, slipped them up inside, began to stroke him. "Quit worrying," she said. "Everything's going to work out fine. Your plan is brilliant. You're going to destroy the Guardians by leading them along the path they've already chosen. What could work better than that?"

He answered her with an unformed little rumble at the back of his throat. One of his hands petted the back of her head urgently. She felt him respond beneath her fingers. Twitching back the single sheet, she bent down to him and opened her mouth.

"Hasn't that bitch said anything yet?" Billy McKay asked around a mouthful of breakfast. The meat was Spam, scarfed from some warehouse or grocery store, but the eggs were fresh. There were plenty of chickens in Tide Camp, brought back when the refugees, under the messianic guidance of Soong, had begun to filter back into the ruins.

"Not yet," Rogers said imperturbably, mopping at egg yolk with a piece of toast.

"Jesus Christ. She's got to know *something*. Isn't it time you started really trying to take her down?"

By now they'd all gotten used to the incongruity of just the four of them sitting around in their fatigues, having breakfast in the huge and echoing state dining room. Heads of state, world leaders who had decided the fates of millions, had dined here. Now they had it all to themselves, four grunts with guns.

Casey and Sam looked off in various directions. "I don't think so, Billy," Tom said.

"I don't much hold with the notion of torturing the

poor woman, even if she is an enemy," Sloan said, still not looking at his chief.

McKay's meaty fist slammed down on the tabletop, making the silverware dance. "God damn it! This is a war we're in. And the President's security is at stake here." He glowered and slurped black coffee. "Besides," he went on, a little quieter, "I ain't suggesting Tom pull her fingers off." *Yet*. "There's other ways of doing it. Hell, we got the drugs to make her think she's Ronald Reagan. We can open her like a can of C-rats."

Sloan looked troubled, but shut up. He and Casey came from a more gentlemanly tradition of war—and also, in a lot of ways, a much more impersonal one. They still had a certain amount of trouble adjusting to ugly realities McKay and Rogers took for granted. What McKay couldn't see was what Tom's problem was.

"I think we should take a little time, handle this right," the former Special Forces soldier said. "She's not going to know anything about individual attacks, even if someone's coordinating them all. There're too many groups involved, and they don't work like that, They're not that organized. For that matter, neither are we. Most of these attacks are pretty spur of the moment."

McKay frowned at his coffee cup. Everything Tom said was true. The sudden rash of attacks on Tide Camp people and their new allies had involved groups ranging from typical juvie gangs such as the Rats and the Razors to the adult Rebel Runners to the guerrilla formations such as the Black Liberation Army. No matter how highly placed their captive was, she wasn't going to be able to pinpoint many attacks for them. Their enemies —hell, most of the bands that crawled and competed in the rubble—were very intuitive, highly unpredictable. Any worthwhile information they were going to drag out of their captive would be more strategic than tactical in nature. Still, the delay griped him.

"Some people just dig in their heels the harder you push them," Rogers went on. "I think she's one of 'em. She'd die before we could force anything out of her. But there are ways around that, like. I'm getting her to talk."

"That ain't been much trouble so far, if you like getting called a fascist a lot."

"No. I mean we're having kind of a dialogue."

"Shit. What, she quotes Chairman Mao at you, and you recite the Pledge of Allegiance?"

Rogers shrugged. "It's a start, Billy."

McKay stared out the window over the South Lawn at the stump of the Washington Monument. *I'm bein' an asshole again, ain't I?* He sighed heavily.

"Awright, Tom. I guess you know what you're doing."

Behind him the Anacostia River flowed sluggish to its rendezvous with the Potomac. Orange firelight twitched across dozens of dirty, attentive faces. *If only my mother could see me now,* Vesensky thought.

For a proper Georgian boy—as if any Russian would admit there was such a thing—he had made quite a spectacle of himself. His pale yellow hair was dyed and greased into a vertical white shock. From his right ear dangled a long panache made of feathers, strips of fur, polished metal bangles; it was balanced by a cuff from which dangled the skull of a rat. A yellow stripe spanned the bridge of his nose beneath eye sockets blacked out so that his green eyes stared forth with mad intensity. Artificial shadows hollowed his cheeks. His lips were black, the bottom one resting on the apex of a scarlet wedge that spread out to encompass the whole of his throat, making him resemble a vampire who was a sloppy eater.

He wore a confection of spikes, chains, and black leather; knee-high black boots with chromed spurs with Mexican rowels the size of dinner plates. To complete the ensemble he had a big CAWS super-shotgun hanging in front of his flat belly by an Israeli-style sling, and a samurai sword which he knew—to a certain extent— how to use slung in its lacquered sheath over his back. To his predominantly youthful audience, he looked as impressive as hell.

Also, none of them would have a hope of recognizing him if and when he decided to shed the role of Witch King of the Ruins.

He only hoped he would neither have to fight nor run in this ridiculous getup. Not that he was unprepared. If he had to split, this location, in a parking lot on the river, had been picked for more than theatrical reasons. In the event of trouble he could simply turn, dash about twenty meters, and dive into the water. A few moments of underwater writhing to rid himself of accoutrements —tricky, but nothing he hadn't done before—and then nothing could possibly catch him except maybe some of those killer dolphins the Kremlin had kept insisting the Americans were secretly training.

If he had to fight, he was backed up by some thirty of Malcolm Jabbar's handpicked bodyguards. They were dressed in black suits, mirror-polished black shoes, and black sunglasses, each armed with an automatic weapon, and he felt the contrast they made with his own heavy-metal psychopath's getup was a deliciously theatrical touch. They weren't, however, there for show. These were Jabbar's storm troopers from before the War, experienced street fighters, trained gunmen, some of whom were vets or former cops. If a pipe blew somewhere, they should be able to mop the waterfront with these leather adolescents, in spite of the kids' armament.

But Vesensky didn't expect that to happen. He had them in his power.

He raised a spiked fist. "*Are you feeling the pressure?*"

A murmur began to ride the sluggish breeze. There were a few muttered assents, a few bobbing heads.

"*I don't hear you. Don't you* know *that the boot is coming down on your necks?*"

"Yeah!" a voice called out loud and clear from the rear. One of Rushton's people, playing the shill right on cue.

"Yeah!" someone else shouted, and another. "Hell yes! *We know!*"

"*And whose boot is it?*"

"Tide Camp."

"This alliance shit."

"Fuckin' Guardians."

"*The Guardians. They've been whipping up the worms. The straights, the settlers, the soft ones. The ones who grovel in the shit to live.*

"*The ones who know your power and fear it!*"

His listeners were no longer hunkered down or flaked out on their asses with affected boredom on their faces. They were up on their feet, waving weapons in the air and hollering, with only a little encouragement from the gnomes he'd planted. He was thankful he'd made himself endure innumerable rock concerts during undercover stints in the West, even though he mostly abominated the music. For hard-core brain-fusing demagoguery, no revolution orator ever born could match a good American or British hard rocker on a roll. Ozone charged the atmosphere; he could smell it as plainly as the ashes and decay and slow rolling water and burning oil and sweat that freighted the humid air.

"And you know why they're doing this?" His voice dropped low, but hummed.

"Why?" they shouted back.

"Why, to make this hellhole safe *for the* President *of the* United States." The wind rolled through a gap in his words. Almost whispered: *"And do you care what happens to the President?"*

"Hell no!"

"Are you going to let them put the clamps on you? Take away your freedom?"

"No!"

". . . because they're trying to. And you know why? Because they're afraid."

The roar of assent almost blew him off his feet. Behind him stood Jabbar's bodyguards, black and immobile and unyielding as monoliths.

"They're afraid! And do they have reason to be?"

"Yes!"

"Are you going to let them put you down? Chain you or drive you from the rubble?"

"No!"

"Then hear me." He threw his arms out to the sides. Behind him the full moon rose over the ruins of Anacostia, enfolding him, silhouetting him like a demon black giant astride the stage that was the world.

"What's in this rubble belongs to him who's strong enough to take it. And we're going to take it. And our time is now."

CHAPTER
FOURTEEN ──────────

Billy McKay stared down at the corpse he'd laid across a heap of broken bricks with a burst from his M-60. "Fuckin' kids."

From somewhere out of sight to his left, 5.56 fire snapped. "Say what, McKay?" Sloan asked in his earphone.

"Nothing." *Asshole*, he told himself. *Letting null bullshit go out over the air*. He'd been through too much to have many problems with shooting someone who'd just fired at him with a shotgun—and damn near hit him, too. Still it was a little bit much when that someone was a girl, and not more than fourteen years old.

Lightning crackle surrounded him. Brick dust swirled about his knees as ricochets tumbled in all directions with plaintive piercing whines. *What the fuck is* wrong *with me?* he wondered as he threw himself down on top of the corpse. Two more goddamn kids, firing him up from behind the stump of a cinderblock wall, while he just stood there with his teeth in his mouth. The only thing that saved him was the fact that even trained troops could rarely hit anything with full-automatic fire from hand-held weapons, even at a range like this.

He could.

Without even bothering to drop the bipod he sprayed bullets at his assailants. One ducked behind the wall. The other stood his ground, doggedly blazing away from the hip. McKay's next burst was aimed, and simply splashed the kid. *At least it's a guy.*

For a moment there was what seemed like silence after the thunder of the guns. McKay lay there trying not to think of the yielding softness beneath him, or what was soaking into the front of his camo coveralls. There were limits to how hard-core even he was, and this was crowding them pretty tight.

"Looks like we got 'em cleaned up, McKay," Sam radioed. *We* were the two Guardians plus members of a band who called themselves the Nuclear Winners, who lived on the edge of the park half a klick or so north of McDaniels's Gold Coast. They had sent a messenger down to the White House to ask for a talk. McDaniels vouched for them, saying they were mainly interested in the universal pastime of scarfing and even, haltingly, doing a little cultivation in Rock Creek Park. So Sloan and McKay had gone out themselves to negotiate.

It was risky, but neither man was exactly afraid to take a chance. Casey and Tom were on call back at the White House to bring Mobile One if needed, even though that would take a while to cover the intervening distance through trashed-out streets. Of more immediate assistance would be Tide Camp's heavy mortar, whose location the Guardians still didn't know. It had an almighty long arm, and packed quite a punch.

The Winners turned out to be a pretty peculiar-looking group of people. But like so many other bedraggled little knots of rubble-crawlers, they were tired of the constant struggle against human predators. Life was tough enough in these ruins.

The brief black muzzle of a CAR-15 poked around the end of the wall and loosed a blind burst. McKay sprayed answering fire a tenth of a meter above the wall's top. "You need a hand, Billy?" Sloan asked, sounding concerned.

"Negative."

The little bastards were brave, McKay had to give them that. They'd attacked the Winners' camp in broad daylight. Some of them had infiltrated a good long distance into their victims' turf. The fight had been short, loud, and vicious. And now it was done, except for one small detail.

"Give up, kid," McKay called. "You ain't got a chance."

Another round-the-corner blast answered him.

This time he put ten rounds right along the top of the wall, hoping to sting the kid with flying grit and sober him up some. "I got you outgunned, and help on the way. I don't want to hurt you. Throw your gun out and come out with your hands up."

A hand flicked into view at the top of the wall. No carbine came over. Instead the round ball of a fragmentation grenade glittered in an arc that ended with a thud in the dust three meters from McKay.

He buried his face in his forearms and tried to make himself two dimensional. The explosion seemed to suffuse him, and he could feel thousands of tiny fragments zipping over him. He was thankful for the special ear inserts the Guardians routinely wore, which protected their eardrums from the damaging effects of nearby gunshots without reducing their sensitivity to lower levels of sound. Without them the drums probably would have gone.

Even before the dust cloud began to fall back McKay had his hands on the machine gun again. *If that's the way he wants to play—* He traversed the barrel to the end of the wall, where it met the sidewalk to his left, begun walking bursts along it at a half-meter height. The heavy copper-jacketed slugs punched right through the brittle cinder block. In a moment he heard a high-pitched scream. He kept punching holes through the block to the end of the wall, waited a beat, and emptied the box walking fire back the other way. He'd had people try to play possum on him before.

He snapped on a new ammo box and rose. The prudent thing to do would be to pitch a grenade, but even though they'd made a stop at one of the caches laid down before the War just prior to hitting Kirtland, and even though there were all kinds of munitions floating around the rubble, there wasn't an endless supply of the things. Instead he moved to the sidewalk and along it, quickly but carefully, trying not to let his rubber boot soles crunch on the grit and gravel. At the last moment he stepped into the street, took several quick steps forward and pivoted.

The kid was sprawled on the floor of a convenience store that had been stripped to its foundation. The little carbine lay several meters away. McKay straightened, approached cautiously.

His caution was strictly pro forma. The kid was unlikely to try any tricks—not with both legs shattered by McKay's first sweep, and a bullet through his chest from the trip back. McKay knelt beside him. Air was sucking in and out of the hole in his chest. That was surprisingly easy to deal with—just slap something nonporous, even a plastic wrapper, over the wound to prevent the lungs collapsing—but McKay made no move to tender first aid. Hemorrhaging in the legs would kill him before the chest wound, and even if McKay could have saved his life, it would have been no kindness to do so. Cripples didn't last long in the rubble.

He cradled the boy's head on his thigh. "Who the hell did this? Who's sending you kids out to die like this?"

The boy opened his eyes. They were big and brown; he had a tan, beaky face. "W-witch King," he croaked.

McKay frowned. "Say what?"

"The wuh . . . Witch King he . . . brought us together. We—we will—wipe you. . . ." The words drifted off. The boy slowly raised a hand, grabbed one of McKay's, clung.

His grip was just relaxing when Sloan and the others came up.

Shadows were reaching into the shattered Treasury Annex and the Court of Claims complex on the east side of Lafayette Park when McKay and Sloan came walking in from their eventful visit to the Winners. A fat gray squirrel clung halfway up the bole of a tree shattered by the Tide Camp barrage and screamed abuse at them.

"Y'know, this park used to hold the largest concentration of those little guys known," Sloan remarked.

McKay gave him a look. "Sometimes I think there's something wrong with you."

Soong's busy elves had installed a gate welded out of lengths of conduit to replace the one knocked down by the mob a year ago. Several warriors stood around shooting the breeze with the guards. It always bugged

McKay to see these dolled-up dudes guarding the White House and, by extension, the President, but there was nothing he could do about it.

Among them was Kerry. He waved cheerfully as the Guardians walked up, across Pennsylvania Avenue.

"Heard you guys saw some action."

McKay grunted. He wasn't feeling very talkative. "Sure did," Sloan said.

They nodded briefly at the guards who swung the gate open for them. Kerry fell into step with them as they started up the drive to the White House. "Bag a lot of the assholes?"

"Jesus," McKay said.

"They were kids," Sloan said. "Just kids."

"I'm sorry." He looked so crestfallen that Sloan felt compelled to try to pump up the conversation and get his mind off his gaffe.

"What's our old friend Diem up to these days?" he asked as they stepped up onto the porch, referring to the Vietnamese kid they'd rescued. Laurie, the girl, was up and around; Sloan had talked to her the day before. She'd seemed to be recovering from her experiences.

A shadow washed across the young man's face. "He's, uh, he's dead."

Sam stopped. "He's what?"

"Dead. He died." His eyes flicked from face to face. "He, never, never—you know—recovered from his wounds—"

McKay slugged him. The kid went staggering back, his Uzi crashing from his hand, eyes pools of hurt, dabbing with the back of his hand at blood spilling over his lower lip.

A couple of Tide Camp bravos lounged on the portico. Before they could react, McKay caught him up by the front of his leather vest and slammed him against a pillar. "That kid wasn't hurt bad. He was barely fucking *scratched*." McKay knew he was exaggerating, but he was upset. "Now, you tell me exactly what happened to him, or I'm going to pound you into this column."

In the old days, the Hell's Angels motorcycle club had a set of bylaws that ran, roughly: (a) in any dispute between Angels and non-Angels, the non-Angels are at fault, and (b) all Angels will participate. Sam Sloan was as shocked by McKay's sudden outburst as anybody, but at the reflex level the Guardians lived by the same code as the Hell's Angels had.

Automatically he stepped to the side and pivoted, getting a pillar against his back and covering the Tide Camp warriors while keeping McKay out of his line of fire. The painted braves stared down the little muzzle of the Galil and the almost two-inch-wide throat of the M-203, and sat very, very still.

The one-time rookie cop wasn't small. McKay was holding him clear of the walkway. "Tell me," he gritted.

"It was—let me breathe." McKay lowered him a millimeter. "He—was up to be made into a warrior. Had to go through the rite of passage. Was—something happened. It was too much for him. He just, his heart gave out."

Tom Rogers materialized in the doorway, Galil ready, drawn by the sounds of dispute and knowing by instinct there was trouble.

"Rite of passage?" McKay bellowed. "What is this shit?"

"O-ordeal," His victim's face was turning purple now; McKay's fist was in his throat. The petrified Kerry managed to shove the words out anyway. "The test of manhood. His heart must have given out, that's all."

"But wait a minute," Sloan said, a look of horror

starting to seep into his face. "Those burns on your chest, when we went on that raid—they were deliberate, weren't they? Jesus, McKay, these people torture their warrior candidates."

McKay's eyebrows rose. "Is that true?"

"Yes."

McKay dropped him. "Shit," he commented, and walked between the other two warriors into the foyer.

"What makes 'em do it, Tom?" McKay asked. They were down in the basement by Mobile One, cleaning their weapons and performing the usual maintenance scutwork under the light of overheads, except for Casey, who was on watch on the top-floor promenade. "I mean, shit, these ain't just a bunch of bikers, scumbags like that. Hell, most of them were soldiers, at least half of 'em saw combat. Lot of them are SF, SEALs, Force RECON, even. Some of them were even Secret Service. Amd yet they're acting like, like a bunch of road gypsies."

"Lack of discipline, Billy," Rogers said from the turret, where he was examining the electrical firing sequences for the two big guns.

"But, hell," McKay said, spraying Break-Free on the parts of the broken-down feed mechanism of his machine gun, "this Soong dude is Special Forces. I'd think he'd keep 'em in hand."

"I'm not sure how much Soong is aware of what goes on with the warriors. I think he mostly goes by what Andy tells him. And Andy can do no wrong."

Sloan rammed a patch down the bore of his Galil. "Are you sure they lack discipline? I have the distinct impression that if one of them steps out of line, our buddy Andy would be more than happy to shoot him on the spot." He shuddered. "Or worse. I mean, they even torture their new recruits."

"It's not the same thing, Sam," Rogers said. "Andy ain't consistent in what sets him off. And a lot of times, he encourages his boys to get wild. You don't call that discipline, do you?" He sounded vaguely reproving.

"Guess not."

Scowling, McKay wiped down the parts of the machine gun. This was really getting into his hide. For real men, real soldiers, to get as crazy as the Tide Camp boys could be . . . maybe it reminded him just a little too much of the old Billy McKay, back in his brawling days before the Guardians.

"Company, Billy," Casey's voice said in his ear. "Andy Aramyan and escorts, figures five, coming up from the Ellipse."

"The grievance committee arrives," Sloan remarked.

McKay threw down his rag and stood up in disgust. "He burns holes in his fucking troopies. What's he care if I punch one some?"

But the battered Kerry was not on Aramyan's mind.

"He died," the Armenian spat without preamble as they met him on the South Portico.

McKay blinked. "I didn't hit him that hard."

Aramyan frowned at him, totally blank, then shook himself all over. "Charles died. I want her."

"Perhaps if you could explain yourself in a little more detail, Lieutenant," Sam suggested gently.

"The driver of the armored car in that ambush. The one who was burned. He died, just now he died. We want the bitch."

"No."

Glowering, Aramyan started to shoulder past.

McKay seemed suddenly to swell and fill the passageway; somehow there wasn't any room past him to either side. "I said no. I meant it. She's a prisoner of the Government of the United States of America. We ain't surrendering her."

"Maybe you should call in the Federal Marshals," sneered one of the shadows backing Aramyan.

"We're the only law east of Dodge, son," Sloan said. "Unless you count the Effsees."

Aramyan's face was almost black in the glow of electric illumination spilling out from the Diplomatic Reception Room at the Guardians' backs. "What are we? Shit?" He sprayed saliva over the front of the fresh fatigue coveralls McKay had changed into before chow. "We're the government too!"

"No, Andy," McKay said, very quietly. "No, you're not. And I'd really suggest you don't forget it."

For a moment they all stood there glaring at each other like samurai in a Japanese adventure flick. Andy's boys were festooned with the usual array of blades, grenades, and autoweapons Tide Campers customarily toted around. The three Guardians had only knives and side arms. Their lone advantage was that Aramyan and company had no way of knowing whether Casey was hiding out of sight somewhere covering them, though in fact he couldn't even see them.

Somehow the moment passed. Andy turned around on the ball of his boot and stalked off. His three bullyboys stood a moment longer, favoring the Guardians with hot-eyed glares of obviously hollow defiance, then followed.

"You know," McKay remarked casually when they were out of earshot, "I'm gonna unscrew that little puke's head for him some day."

McKay came awake in a luxurious second-floor bedroom filled with rosy morning sun, half out of bed and groping for this M-60. He knew at once what had awakened him. *Gunfire. Not all that far away.*

"McKay here. We under attack?"

"Rogers here. Negative, Billy. Seems to be a klick or two to the east."

"Roger. Glad I don't have to go to war in my skivvies." That was one problem with the issue Guardians coveralls; they were a bitch to get into in a hurry.

As he dressed more reports came in. Sloan, monitoring Tide Camp traffic on the radio, relayed word that there seemed to be fighting around Capitol Hill. "Small arms, grenades, maybe even rockets."

The bedframe rattled to a distant *crump*. "I can hear 'em from here. You and Case shag ass down to Mobile One and saddle up. We gotta be ready to move out if they start moving this way."

Fully dressed, he had picked up his machine gun and started for the door when Sloan came back over the commnet. "We just got a call from Seth Rushton. He's under heavy attack from the BLA, and he's screaming for help so loud he barely needs a radio."

CHAPTER
FIFTEEN ——————————

"Casey, hit the brakes." Stacked in the turret behind the two main guns, Tom Rogers sounded almost urgent. With cobra reflexes Casey Wilson jammed on the brake. Half a heartbeat later a LAW rocket buzzed past, drawing a thick brushstroke of white smoke not three meters from Mobile One's front glacis.

Servos whirred as the turret swung left. Through the glass-and-plastic-laminate vision blocks Rogers saw a thin white dude standing in a blown-out show window, the stubby tube of an expended launcher just coming off his shoulder, his face twisting into an expression of angry frustration at having missed such a big, juicy target. Other figures moved frantically behind him, trying to relocate in a hurry.

He seemed to be coming out of his fuzz when a 40-mm High Explosive Dual Purpose grenade hit him in the sternum and he simply vanished from eyebrows to belt buckle in a gush of orange flame. Two other grenades flashed off among his buddies behind as his legs crumpled, spurting blood.

Casey goosed the big car. It bucked the curb and took off across what had been a park, the tire cleats tearing out mouthfuls of turf. The expanse of shin-high grass was a sort of wing projecting north from the Mall to the sprawling shambles of Union Station, an even bigger mess than it had been before the One-Day War.

Ten metric tons of V-450 shouldered aside a couple of trees in a stand set on high ground. Rogers traversed the turret again, bringing its armament to bear down a mere hundred meters of slope toward a low point, currently swampy, east of the Taft Memorial, from which a score of men and women were spraying fire at Capitol Hill. The M-19 going off and the aggressive blatting of its diesel engine had caught their attention even over a brisk firefight. Some of them jumped up and started running east or west even as Rogers opened up with the Browning .50 caliber.

They were a little late.

The Roman-nosed Mercedes flatbed truck lay on its side, burning. Billy McKay hauled ass for the side of the street, dragging a badly injured Tide Camper by his leather harness. Apparently the team he and Sloan had been leading up toward the park south of the Rayburn Building hadn't been making quick enough progress for Andy Aramyan's tastes. The big Merc had come charging past them down Delaware Avenue, snorting like an angry bull. Then some kind of rocket—McKay guessed an RPG-7, a Soviet-block tank buster—had cracked out of nowhere and smacked that sucker head-on. The truck went over like a rhino hit with a .600 Nitro Express.

Ten meters to McKay's right Sloan stepped out of a doorway, popped a round out of the M-203 launcher slung under his assault rifle's barrel, stepped back as the round landed at the head of the block with a dropped-cantaloupe sound and filled the end of the street with thick white smoke. McKay heaved up his Maremont, triggered a one-handed burst down the block into the swirling tear gas, just for the John Wayne of it. Then he dragged the wounded man into a building he'd seen several other Tidal Basin braves duck into.

He found himself in the lobby of one of the area's innumerable government agencies. He let his burden down on a maroon carpet, which was now worn as thin as a sheet of paper. One of the men who had accompanied him and Sloan emerged from a stairway to his left, a wiry Oriental-looking guy with an OD rag tied around his temples, black muscle shirt with a skull and crossbones design in white flaking off the front, camouflage pants—positively drab by Tide Camp standards. He was carrying an old Garand, for God's sake, damn near as long as he was. "Building's clear," he reported.

"Medic around?"

"I can fake it."

McKay nodded, moved back toward the entrance.

Between outbursts of hysteria, the Guardians had been able to garner an impressionistic picture of the disaster that had befallen Rushton and his American Union people. They claimed a major chunk of central Washington turf, stretching from Union Station in the north, Fourth street to the east, Route 395 to the south, and the National Gallery of Art and the Air and Space Museum on opposite sides of the Mall—the rest of the Smithsonian being no man's land between Union and Tide Camp. Rushton had not been just horribly eager to let his new allies know too much about his strength or its dispositions, but from Andy's surprisingly efficient intelligence service they gathered he somehow managed to support several hundred people. Of course, fewer than half of those could come close to counting as combat strength, and McKay was none too sure how elite any of Rushton's people were as warriors.

On the other hand, they had managed to grab this chunk of real estate and hang on to it for the better part of a year, so they couldn't be total screw-offs. Nonetheless, their attackers didn't seem to have encountered much trouble infiltrating by night, because they had suddenly opened fire on the outlying positions from the rear with the break of day. Rushton's defense lines had collapsed like Third World currency until he found himself surrounded on the Hill with a goodly portion of his people dead, captured, or bugged out.

Just who the enemy was, wasn't any too clear. The Black Liberation Army was in on this party—McKay's team had killed a man with the BLA's distinctive red-green-black flag patch sewn on his jacket not a block away. But from the kaleidoscopic impressions he'd gotten, plus reports from Tom and Casey, the Tide Camp troopies, and Rushton's embattled people, it looked like a real cross-section of vermin had come crawling out of sewers for this one. Predominantly white kid gangs and runner packs were mixing with black terrorists. It was like the lion lying down with the lamb, although that never suggested anything to McKay but one lucky lion.

There was no breeze, and in the usual morning heat Sloan's CS screen cordoned off the end of the block like a fluffy white wall. *Great, but this ain't relieving Rushton*. McKay unshipped his gas mask from its carrier on his belt and stepped into the street, ready to push on.

Another Basin troopie came trotting up to him from down the block. "We're taking heavy fire from the House Office complex. Lieutenant Aramyan's authorized a fire mission for the four-deuce, sir."

"Real good of you to tell us. Sloan, did you get that? They're gonna fire their big gun."

"Big gun? In the Navy, the lifeboats carry bigger guns than four point two inches."

"Very fucking funny. Just hope that mother doesn't drop one short, Mr. Black-Shoe Commander Sloan. You ain't got a foot of armor plating over your pointy head."

McKay faded back into the office building and took up station behind a window to cover the street with his M-60 and wait for the bombardment. He wished he could find something decent to prop the hog on a meter or so inside, so he wouldn't have to hang its barrel over the sill—a trick generally reserved for half-wits and Hollywood heroes—but there was nothing. Shots seemed to be coming and going all around him. *Somebody's busting a lot of caps.*

"Incoming, Billy," came Casey Wilson's voice, relaying the word from the Tide Camp mortar pits. For a man used to the multiplex tasks involved in piloting a modern fighter aircraft, a simple task like driving an armored car into battle while monitoring your ostensible allies' radio traffic on the side was a piece of cake.

A handful of heartbeats later McKay heard a familiar freight train rushing overhead.

"For God's sake," Marcie FitzAllen said in disgust. "Do you idiots have to just stand there waiting for a stray shot to hit you?"

Of the three, only the man who called himself Ian Victor spared her a glance and quick smile where she lay behind a sandbag. Malcolm Jabbar, looking cool despite the heat in a black turtleneck and dark gray trousers, just stood there, with Seth practically hopping

from one foot to the other side beside him in excitement, watching it all unfold from the ground floor of
the Capitol's southern wing.

"Not a lot to worry about, my dear," Victor said.
"Most of that's happening on a plane below ours, so to
speak."

"I've never heard so much macho bullshit in my
life."

Victor laughed. She was right. Another big mortar
round socked the Rayburn Building. Even up here the
clatter of fragments rebounding off the masonry all
around sounded like a flurry of hail.

"A brilliant conception, Seth," Jabbar murmured.
For all the overt praise in his words, they were edged
with ice. 'You convince our friends in the Tidal Basin of
our good faith, at the same time you persuade them to
reveal the location of their heavy artillery. Brilliant."

Rushton gave him a watery grin. "It's mostly Ian's
idea, really."

"Indeed."

Indeed it was a setup. In his role as the Witch King it
had been no problem for Vesensky to whip up the attack. Knowing the plan, Rushton had pulled back all of
his people except for a few sacrificial pickets for
verisimilitude's sake. In the BLA stalwarts, best-trained
and best-disciplined elements in that disparate attack
force, the planners had perfect sheepdogs to make sure
things moved the way they wanted them to.

That this elaborate scheme would entail spilling a fair
amount of their own side's blood didn't much faze
anyone.

"You can't make an omelette without breaking
eggs," Seth Rushton had repeatedly pointed out;
Nathalie Frechette wasn't the only one addicted to that
cliché.

Another mortar round crashed home. The onlookers felt a brief hot breeze push against their faces. To the south a flare soared up over the ruins of Fort McNair, a hot bright point burning a hole in hazy summer sky.

"They've done it! They've spotted the mortar." Rushton was practically jumping up and down in excitement.

Vesensky looked at Jabbar. "Do you think your men can pull out successfully?"

Jabbar looked back coolly. "Of course. Can yours?"

Vesensky shrugged. It didn't matter that much. His zealots were disposable.

"So now we start making noise, demanding a summit meeting," Marcie asked, still behind her sandbags.

"Oh, no," Vesensky said. "I don't fancy you'll have to do that at all. Given what happened today, and the pressure we've been putting on our friends' other allies, I doubt we'll have to be the ones to broach the subject. Of course, once it comes up, Seth will be most vocal calling for it to take place as soon as possible. Malcolm, on the other hand, will require persuasion. Satisfactory, gentlemen?"

"Oh, yes, yes," Rushton said.

"Yes," said Jabbar, looking very closely at Seth Rushton.

The sun had set by the time the four Guardians rolled back through the White House gates. Once Tide Camp's big mortar ended the discussion, the assault had collapsed in a hurry, which wasn't surprising, since nothing strained morale as badly as an artillery barrage. Even the single, if relatively large, tube was more than sufficient to scatter the ragtag attackers, no matter how cunning they'd been infiltrating in the first place.

Once it was apparent the heat was off, the Guardians

left. They wanted to check on their other allies, lend them assistance if they too had come under attack, at least reassure them. Mopping up was Rushton's job, and it looked as though he was going to have all the assistance he needed from Andy Aramyan's wild boys.

None of the Guardians' other allies, from the Gold Coast to the kid gangs, had been attacked for twenty-four hours, for some an unexpected respite. After the fact it wasn't too mysterious, since it was clear the Witch King or the BLA or whoever had masterminded the attack on the Capitol had spent the time mustering and positioning the attacking forces.

News traveled fast in the rubble. Everyone knew Rushton had been hit, and hard. As was to be expected, rumor grossly exaggerated both the extent of the attack and its damage. But the core of it all, that some kind of coalition of rubble badasses had jumped on the Union, was dead on. The message was clear: they were facing an ever-more-organized enemy, while their own organization remained largely hypothetical.

"We gonna have an alliance, it's about time we started to meet some of our *allies*," the warlord of the Bloods summed up succinctly. "So far all we got is talk, and four honkies in an armored car. Now, that's a mighty fine armored car, but ain't no armored car can be two places at once."

From the Georgetown Boys to the Nuclear Winners, there was startling unanimity; if there was going to be any kind of alliance it had to come together now.

Late in the afternoon the Guardians swung back by the Capitol, where the action had died down. A disheveled Rushton was only too eager to go along with the idea of a meeting. Less convinced was Jabbar, who had shown up with some of his personal bodyguards in their distinctive black turtlenecks as reinforcements in the middle of the afternoon. He was distinctly cool to the notion, but Rushton took McKay aside and assured him that if the meeting took place, he would personally see that Jabbar attended. McKay didn't trust Rushton to cross the street unaided, but he didn't say anything. He wasn't exactly going to pout if Jabbar didn't show.

The Guardians themselves wanted very little as much as such a meeting. But it was going to be a son of a bitch. They had to find a place to do it and get it all together and soon, before some of their shakier allies bolted.

The rubble crawlers had had a busy little year, and a number of the groups they had tied into their network had built up some pretty brisk enmities among themselves; coordinating the whole thing was going to be child's play compared with keeping some of these people from going for one another on sight. Nonetheless, the sudden clamor for a summit conference was their first big break toward making Washington safe for the President.

The Tide Camp guards on duty at the North Lawn gate seemed flushed, excited, and McKay wondered if they hadn't celebrated the Capitol Hill victory with some chemical refreshment. They didn't have much to say, though, just waved Mobile One through and shut the gate again.

"Going to check on our captive?" Sam Sloan asked as Casey steered the big car down the ramp to the sub-terranean garage.

"You making any progress, Tom?" Casey asked.

"He spends any more time in there with her, we're going to have to move a cot in for him," McKay said as Casey pulled to a stop and the heavy remote-control doors chopped off the light behind them. "Or maybe not. I think they got something going, myself.''

Rogers said nothing. He was not the type to respond to the usual teasing banter. But for all his skill as an interrogator, he was stymied. Once Uhuru Assad had realized the shocking fact of her captivity, loss of freedom—an experience unlike any she'd ever known before—she had fallen in on herself like a dynamited building. Instead of political diatribes alternating with shrieked imprecations, she now communicated in sullen grunts, if at all.

Nevertheless, he continued to insist that the deliberate method was best. For one thing, their captive was obviously very intelligent and probably fairly important to their enemy. She could be very valuable to them, provided they employed interrogation techniques that left her intact.

In the week since her capture, McKay had made frequent noises about bearing down. That was just McKay being McKay. No matter what they said about being able to break anybody, McKay knew a really good interrogation took time. From his own extensive experience in the field, much of it less than savory, he knew full well that torture didn't always produce useful results. Once you started carving on somebody, what they told you was what they thought you wanted to hear, what would make you stop. And occasionally you did find someone who would just plain die or go round the bend before cracking. If Tom said that this was the way to play it, that was enough for him.

He went up to check on MacGregor. Jeff was spending most of his time reading books from the White House library and fretting. These days he didn't have much to do but brood about the fact that he was a President in name only. He seemed distracted, barely listened when McKay reported the day's activities. Unusually thoughtful, McKay excused himself and walked out of the office.

To bump into Tom Rogers in the corridor. He looked like death itself. "She's gone," he said.

"What?"

"While we were gone somebody snuck in and took the girl."

"Three guesses who." McKay undid the flap on his Kevlar holster, pulled out his .45, dropped the magazine, checked it, slammed it back home. "Gather round, boys. We got to pay us a social call."

CHAPTER
SIXTEEN ——————————————

Andy's boys had her.

They had a couple of long, perforated-metal poles, of the type used to put up street signs, planted in the trampled turf of the terrace to the right of the Lincoln Memorial's steps and lashed together in the center in the form of a large X. Wired to the X by wrists and ankles was Uhuru Assad. She was naked. Her wiry body glistened and her pubic hair was matted with some sort of fluid. Her eyes rolled wildly from right to left at the half-circle of gaudy warriors who thronged around, jeering, brandishing torches.

Onto the terrace stalked Andy Aramyan, his hands clasped over his head like a champion boxer. The mob cheered. "We got the bitch who burned Charley, don't we?" A growl answered him. "And we're gonna make her burn tonight. *Aren't we?*"

The howling response was cut short by a snarl of machine gun fire that stitched earth in front of the toes

of Andy's jungle boots and bounced big divots of turf
off the knees of his cammie pants.

"Everybody out of the pool," Bill McKay said, step-
ping out from behind a fat pillar at the corner of the
Monument with a cigar in his face and his Maremont
M-60 in his hands. "The party's over."

Everybody stared at him, Andy with his eyebrows
pulled together into one thick black line and his mouth
hanging open in a comical O of surprise. Then another,
more compact figure slipped onto the cleared area with
Andy. Tom Rogers, cool and casual as if going for a
stroll around the basin to look at the cherry trees, but
with his Galil Short Assault Rifle held at an angle across
his flat belly, ready for instant action. "Cut her down,
Andy," he said, "and we'll forget about all this."

Aramyan's fingers cramped into fists, and the veins
stood out on his forearms. He was trembling all over.
"What do you do?" he shrieked. "*How dare you?*"

McKay smiled. "Cause we got the drop on you,
Andy."

"The fuckers're bluffing!" screamed a big dude with
electric red sideburns. "There's just two of them. What
the fuck can they do?"

"Ask your buddy Tyler if he thinks we're the type to
bluff." The skinny squad leader who'd led them to the
kidnappers' hideout dropped his eyes. "You took our
prisoner. We've come to take her back. And if you
pukes should get lucky and grease the two of us, Sam
Sloan's got a bead with his M-19 right on old Andy.
He'll chop you to pieces and fry those for bacon. You
dig?"

He surveyed the mob, wondering if they had a hope in
hell of pulling this off. The stench of gasoline rammed
up his nose and into his sinuses like steel fingers. *These
pukes are serious.*

He caught sight of a face in the front rank, familiar once his mind stripped away the greasepaint and the feathers. "Well, if it ain't my old buddy Bill Madden. And here I thought you were the sane one in the group."

Madden studied the turf.

"Well, good buddy, you just tell these little pals of yours that if you don't play nice, I'm gonna say the magic words, 'Almighty, Almighty, this is PBR Street Gang' and things is gonna get *real* interesting."

Andy gave one last convulsive shake and went limp, standing with his head hanging slack on his neck. "Burn, baby, burn," screamed the giant with red whiskers. He turned, grabbed a torch from a man standing next to him, cocked back an arm to throw it.

Tom Rogers snapped a shot from the hip. A little nailhead hole appeared above the redhead's right eyebrow, his cheek popped and his eyes bulged out as catastrophic overpressure pulped his brain, and he went right down. The torch sizzled ineffectually at green grass.

In dead silence the crowd backed away, none more rapidly than several who had had the big man's brains blown all over them. But there's one in every crowd, and this one shouted from the rear, "They shot Verle! The fuckers killed him!" Then with a sound that came from very low in about sixty throats, the mob started forward again, unlimbering weapons with a rustle like a lot of metal cockroaches.

Rogers glided to Aramyan's side, yanked one arm up behind him in a hammerlock and stuck the flash suppressor of his Galil into the little trap formed by the confluence of ear, jaw, and neck. Billy McKay clamped the black steel buttplate of the M-60 against his ribs and got ready to die a lot.

"This is gonna ruin everybody's day," he said.

"Stop!" A voice boomed like an evening gun. "Stop, all of you! Stop this at once."

Moving through the crowd like an icebreaker came Soong himself. When they realized their leader was among them, the painted bravos melted back. A couple didn't move quick enough, and bounced mighty hard when he ran into them.

Soong stepped into the cleared semicircle before the terrace, stood with his bare feet planted wide, his nostrils flared. He stared up at the naked woman on the cross. "My god," he breathed.

"What's going on, Billy?' Sloan asked over the communicator. "Do you need help?"

"Negative. I think the cavalry just showed up."

Rogers let his Galil slip away from Andy's neck, pushed the man away from him, stood with weapon in patrol position, muzzle down, respectfully attentive but still alert. His face was as impassive as a Buddha.

Andy shook his head, quickly, like a terrier killing a rat, then charged up to his boss. "They're murderers!" he screamed. "They killed—"

Soong swiveled his great head and looked at him. Andy winced back as if struck, the word flow ceasing instantly. His leader turned his bulk around to face the crowd of warriors.

"Are we really animals, then," he asked, his voice pitched to carry, "or are we men? We have fought to preserve an island of peace and justice in the midst of chaos. We now have the chance to bring those things to the great gaping wound that was the capital of our nation. How can we let ourselves descend to"—he raised a great hand at the cross behind him, starkly outlined against the Monument's white face—"this?"

The crowd had begun to fall back, eyes downcast,

murmuring like so many sullen children. "It's justice," Andy whined, not looking at his chief. "She led an ambush where several of us died. Charley Douglas died from burns. We thought—you know—this would be appropriate—"

"Even so, this is not the right way."

Standing off to one side on the shoulder of the slope, McKay wished it was safe to light a cigar. *Looks like we ain't gonna be playing Little Big Horn after all.* The enormous Secret Service man seemed genuinely shocked by the proceedings. But McKay doubted this was the first time Andy and the boys had played games with captives. *Bet there's a lot of things old Soong don't know go on.*

"Was she not a prisoner of our good friends, the Guardians?" Soong asked.

Andy nodded. "But they weren't doing anything." The whine crept up the scale. "They were just keeping her there in the White House, coddling her as if she had not done damn all! We wanted justice!"

The great head nodded at the girl, cringing and shivering, skin showing goosebumps beneath her coating of gasoline. "And this you call justice?"

He shook his head, turned to face the warriors who were nominally his. "A great wrong has been done here. A greater one narrowly averted. It is unfortunate that one of us had to die, but that is the price we sometimes pay for action without thought. Go, all of you; go, and we will forget this ever happened."

They're never gonna buy it, McKay thought, surreptitiously improving his grip on the M-60. But, astonishingly, they did. The heavily armed bravos in the paint and feathers began to drift away, the crowd eroding like a clump of turf in a swift-moving stream.

Tom Rogers slung his Galil, drew his Ka-bar and used

it to cut the wire that bound the young woman's right arm. It had cut cruelly into her flesh, and her wrists and ankles were bloody, her fingers and toes swollen. She watched him with dull eyes as if not even seeing him, then collapsed unconscious across him as he worked on her second hand. He braced her with one arm while he finished the work, then pulled her into a fireman's carry. "Better bring Mobile One, Casey. She's in pretty bad shape."

"Roger." Casey, who'd been covering the whole thing with his sniper's rifle from the upper story of the Academy of Sciences, slipped back down to the concealed car.

The warriors were wandering off across the grass into West Potomac Park, leaving only Andy Aramyan standing with lowered eyes before his boss. Soong sighed, dropped a hand onto the man's shoulder, squeezed gently, "Ah, Andy." Andy turned and walked swiftly, stiffly away.

Soong turned up the slope. "Gentlemen, I am sorry. I hope the young woman has not been harmed."

"I don't think she's got any permanent damage, at least not physical," Rogers said.

McKay walked up to them. "Thanks for lending us a hand, Captain."

"It was the least I could do. You are doing so much for us, for all the people of this country. And we must maintain civilized standards of behavior among ourselves, no matter how hard it sometimes is." Rogers and McKay gave each other a look, but said nothing.

"Please don't judge Andy too harshly, my friends. He is a good man, but sometimes he lets his temper get the better of him."

She was sitting on the dining hall–style table in her

room with her legs drawn up when Tom Rogers entered the room that served as her cell. She held very still, watching him with eyes that seemed as big as a child's. He walked over and propped himself against the table beside her.

If he was aware she wasn't wearing anything under the man's shirt they'd given her—one of Wild Bill Lowell's, last official occupant of the place—he gave no sign. When they'd brought her in several hours before he had given her an examination as thorough and impersonal as any doctor. But this was different now, and both knew it.

"How are you doing?" he asked, not looking at her.

A laugh like glass breaking. "Hey, I'm fine. What could be wrong with me?" She almost kept her voice steady.

She was coiled like a spring, ready to hurl herself in any direction. But he made no move, said nothing. "So, what is this?" she asked. "The hero saves the girl in peril, she supposed to throw herself at him in gratitude, right?"

She pivoted, toes pointed, balletic, lay herself full length on the cool formica, slowly drew her knees apart. "Well, go ahead, big boy. Here's your reward."

He looked at her without a flicker of lust, of recognition even, in those shark-gray eyes.

"What's the matter?" she taunted. "Isn't this what you came for?"

"I thought you might want to talk."

She drew her legs down, folded up onto her knees. "You came to pump me, you honky motherfucker!"

Her hand flashed for his larynx, edge stiffened to a blade. He blocked it, backhanded her. She slumped back against the wall, glaring like a leopard.

"That's what turns you on, huh, big man?"

He made no response.

Suddenly she was weeping. She lunged for him, not attacking, clinging to him, convulsed by sobs. He put one arm around her shoulders and held her firmly until she cried herself out.

"Thank you for not letting them burn me," she finally said in a small voice.

He continued to hold her in silence.

"You really don't expect me to fuck you because you rescued me?" she asked, wondering, no longer cynical.

"No."

She shook her head. "Seems like all the men I've known expected to be paid with sex. Or expected me to prove myself by putting out. Even—" She broke off. "I think maybe I've been a fool. Or maybe I'm being a fool now. I don't know; I don't know anything anymore. A few days ago I was so certain how everything was. Now—" She shook her head. "I don't know. I feel as if I've come all apart, like everything I was so sure of—"

She drew away, pulled down the hem of the shirt in an incongruously girlish gesture. "I guess I'm running on."

"Happens. You been through a bad time."

"You don't bend, Mister, do you? But you don't push, either." She let her legs swing over the edge of the table, bare feet swinging freely. "Maybe this is all a trick. Mutt and Jeff, the old good cop/bad cop routine. Maybe you got tired of talking to me, listening to me with my dialectics and debate."

She smiled, suddenly, unsteadily. "If so, I guess it's worked. You ain't what I thought, and nothing's as I thought it was."

His gaze rested on her, cool and dry as stone. She stared at the carpet and wrung her hands as if washing them. "I can't tell you everything. I won't give up my main man. Maybe my political convictions weren't as ironbound as I thought, but this is personal."

She rubbed her eyes, smoothed her short hair down at the sides of her head.

"You've probably guessed these attacks aren't coincidental. They're being planned and coordinated by a dude who pulled into town a couple of weeks ago. Some of the brothers had had contact with him before. He is a very heavy dude. A real Soviet agent, bona fide. He's raising an army in the rubble—"

"Vesensky," McKay said in the darkness.

Tom nodded. They were up on the promenade, where McKay was taking his turn on watch. It was a routine they hadn't practiced since coming to terms with Tide Camp, but somehow, tonight, they weren't feeling too trustful of their allies.

"She don't know his name, but that's who it has to be. He's using the Black Liberation Army for cadre, but he seems to be passing himself off as a messianic figure, some kind of heavy metal hero."

"*He's* the Witch King?"

"Looks like it."

McKay stared off south to where moonlight glinted off the Tidal Basin. "Holy shit," he said softly. It was all there was to say.

The next two days were tense in the White House. McKay was royally pissed at Tom Rogers, but there was no way he could even say anything. He didn't, when all was said and done, have anything to be pissed about.

Tom's delaying tactics had worked, after all. They'd finally gotten answers from their captive; maybe one more answer than they'd bargained for.

But Marshal Commander Uhuru Assad hadn't totally

turned her coat. She had decided the Guardians were her friends—or rather, that Tom was—and she was trying to steer a line between helping them and harming her former comrades. And, after all, was it such big news that Vesensky himself was on their case? He was Maximov's number-one ferret, and the Washington rubble was just the kind of rathole he worked best in. Deep inside McKay had never doubted he'd be sent in after them.

Whereas he had a gut feeling that it was one of the pieces of data she was holding out on them that they really needed.

But that wasn't what ticked him off. It just rankled McKay's ass that they'd almost got right up against it with their major allies in the rubble, the people actually guarding the White House grounds, over some goddamned terrorist. If Tom had just wrung her out and tossed her to the wolves of Tide Camp, that would have been that and they never would have had to know what they did with her. Instead, Tom had insisted on playing Mr. Nice Guy, and it had almost come down to the Alamo.

They'd never had any choice but to face off with Andy and his gang. Because the issue wasn't the terrorist bitch, not that at all. The Guardians were fighting to restore the authority of the President and Government of the United States. The Tide Camp warriors had defied that authority, sneaking into the White House while the President was occupied and Dr. Srinarampa off visiting his new pal Soong, jimmying the lock of the captive's cell and carting her off.

That was too direct a challenge. It could not be allowed to happen. So the Guardians had had to risk blowing up everything they'd worked for in a bloody no-win showdown with what was supposed to be their own team.

And that asshole Aramyan hadn't even let them play nice. If he'd just been able to hold off a little bit before trying to turn the captive into a bonfire, then Sam and Tom would have had time to negotiate, cool things down, work something else. But no. Instead Andy had gone dashing off, triumphantly clutching the woman like a kid who's just raided the cookie jar under his mom's nose, and just couldn't wait to stick her up almost in sight of the White House and light her off like a belated Fourth of July celebration.

The Guardians had no room for maneuvering. There was nothing to do but move quickly and decisively— risking a radiotelephone call to Soong in his quarters on the island—and then face-off like something out of the Old West. And blood had been spilled, and that was going to be bad blood between Tide Camp and the Guardians.

But McKay had no time to sit on his ass and moan. Things were getting very tight all around. Scarf parties foraging among the ruins were getting bushwhacked regularly. The allies were getting hit on their own turf, from sporadic sniping and harassing fire with rockets— which also served to demonstrate that the Guardians' big iron machine was a long way from invincible—to full-scale nocturnal raids.

One thing the Guardians had been able to provide was a modicum of radio communications with their various allied factions. Most civilian electronics had been trashed by EMP, so working radios weren't easy to scarf. However, by the time of the One-Day War a lot of higher-end civilian electronics had been built around silicon-lattice or gallium-arsenide semiconductors, which resisted electromagnetic pulse, and some of these were available. More to the point, the D.C. police, as well as the vast array of federal agencies, had largely converted to EMP-resistant communications, so some groups had managed to get hold of functional radios anyway, and there were more than enough spare units in the White House itself to equip the rest, at least well enough to maintain touch with the powerful and sensitive broadcasting/receiving setup in the White House.

Even though two Guardians had to be on duty at the White House at all times after the confrontation at the Lincoln Memorial, just in case the Tide Camp bravos got any ideas, Tom Rogers was able to continue some of his hearts-and-minds work on the side. He'd given some quick seminars in forward observation, so that the night after the showdown with Andy the Super Machos had been able to call down fire from the Tide Camp mortar to bust up a fairly serious attack. The Tidal warriors may have taken to regarding the Guardians in hot-eyed, angry silence, but there was no controversy at all when it came to killing bad guys.

McKay had been busy, making rounds and talking to people. As if putting together the summit conference wasn't tricky enough, there was the problem of security. The leaders of every faction involved in the alliance, including the Guardians and Tide Camp, were going to be gathered together in one place. If Vesensky was the intelligence behind the outbreaks of violence, he couldn't hope for a more inviting target.

Strangely enough, finding a neutral ground to meet on was no problem. The problem was that the choice was so obvious that this damned Witch King, Vesensky or not, would have no trouble guessing where the meeting was going to come off. So the big secret was when.

Rogers and McKay hand-delivered to the chief, head man, warlord, or whatever of every allied faction a sealed envelope. He—or she in a couple of cases—was told to guard it with his or her life, not let anyone even know of its existence. From the White House they had already begun to broadcast strings of nonsense words at odd hours of the day; their allies were to monitor those broadcasts. If, at a certain time in the evening they heard a certain phrase that the Guardians made them commit to memory, they were to open the envelope. It contained the location of the meeting and what personnel could attend; the code phrase would mean it was all happening the next morning.

McKay and Rogers had wanted notification to go out no earlier than the morning of the meeting. But Seth Rushton, among others, had said he needed more time to get ready. Leaving it overnight was just begging the enemy to find out when and where the meeting would take place. But the Guardians were acutely aware that there was only a certain extent to which they could dictate to their fiercely independent allies. Reluctantly they had to give in and hope for the best.

McKay didn't think they were going to get it.

She looked up from the book she was reading, crosslegged on the nondescript carpet, when Tom came in. "Hi," she said, smiling.

Tom nodded. "Evening. What you reading?"

"*Marxism*. By a black dude, Thomas Sowell. Casey got it for me out of the library." She closed it in her lap. She was wearing scarfed jeans and another of Wild Bill's dress shirts. "A pretty together guy, this Sowell. Started off as a Marxist himself, but he decided that had some problems with it. He's kind of turning my head around."

Tom sat in a stained antique chair. "Glad you ain't bored."

"Meaning you would be, if you had to try to wade through some kind of political-analysis treatise?" She stood up and came to his chair, laughing. "Mr. Rogers, I wonder if you maybe do have a sense of humor hiding down inside there." She shook her head. "Listen to this shit. 'Mr. Rogers.' I just can't see you saying, 'Can you say that? I knew you could.' "

He sat looking at her, feeling no need to speak, making no apology for the fact. A mass at rest, perfectly balanced.

"Sometimes I think you can look right through to the middle of me with those eyes of yours," she said in a voice just slightly afraid.

She leaned down and kissed him.

"Maybe I'm looking for a father figure. Or maybe I need some kind of center, some kind of solidity, and you're the most solid thing I've ever seen, Tom Rogers." She kissed him again.

This time he responded, and then his arms were around her, pulling her to him with crushing force.

Later, they lay side by side on the mattress resting on the carpet, which served as her bed. She ran a finger across his chest. "Looks like the lunar landscape. Where you been to get banged up like this, Mr. Tom?"

"Around."

She laughed. "I never thought of myself as the kind to go for the strong, silent type. Guess it goes to show you never know."

"Signal went out tonight. Meeting's tomorrow morning." Her fingers froze against a long curving scar that twined among the hair on his chest. Her eyes slid away from his. "Is there anything else you can tell me?"

She rolled over, away from him. "No." Her body was rigid, lightly trembling.

She felt the mattress shift as he sat up, stood. She lay staring, unseeing, as he dressed. Then he leaned down, kissed her high cheekbone in front of her ear. "G'night."

He went out. She stared at the door for a long, long time.

"Is everything ready?" Seth Rushton's words echoed up to the top of the Rotunda dome. Outside it was nearly dawn; in here it was almost cool. Rushton was fidgeting, striving manfully to contain his impatience.

The lights glowed low at the impulse of hidden generators. Marcie was there, and Jabbar with some of his sleek black wolves with their folding-stock AKs slung by their sides.

"Everything," said Ivan Vesensky. He was wearing his high-heeled boots and his spikes and leather Witch King drag, but had not yet applied the makeup. "Our people are already in position. This is the *pièce de reśistance*—which I prepared myself." Professional that he was, he still had to smile.

"And that greasy little Greek tycoon?" Marcie asked, stepping forward. "What about him? He's liable to make trouble."

"No, he's not," Jabbar said in that stick-dry voice of his. "We've placed certain of his family members under, ah, protective custody. He's only too eager to cooperate."

Rushton rubbed his hands together. "This is splendid! The last stumbling blocks are about to be cleared from our path. Soon we'll restore the flow of consumer goods to the working people of America."

"No doubt," Malcolm Jabbar murmured, "but you won't be there to see it."

Rushton blinked. Without his knowing it, the scene had somehow slipped out of focus. Suddenly there were black men to either side of him, their fingers gripping him like steel pincers behind the elbow, making his hands go numb with pain. And the others were slipping back to the walls to cover the few other Union people in the great hall. Vesensky stood by, a small frown on his face. And Marcie was gliding to Jabbar's side, his hand going around her hip.

"A-aren't you going to do something, Ian?" Words rasped from his throat like gravel.

"This is perhaps a trifle premature, is it not, Malcolm?"

Anger flashed briefly in Jabbar's hooded eyes. It was quickly suppressed. Jabbar was no fool. He knew perfectly what "Ian Victor" was, knew that the handful of his gunslingers in the Rotunda were a long ways from enough to ensure Jabbar would walk away if he called the blond man's bluff.

He made himself say smoothly, "Perhaps. I'll make his excuses for him at the meeting. And soon it won't matter." Thinking, *Someday, you supercilious ofay piece of shit. Someday.* "Take him away and stick him someplace. I may have use of him later."

The two bodyguards began to hustle Rushton away. "Marcie, why?" he choked. "Is it because—because—" Even in his extremity he couldn't form the words. Betraying him for some black prick?

She shook her head. "It has nothing to do with that, Seth," she said. "It's just because you're such a nerd."

CHAPTER
SEVENTEEN ─────────────

It was a murky day. The sky looked like cooked oatmeal, and the air felt like it. "Park her anyplace around here, Casey," Billy McKay said. "We hump it from here."

The big armored car shuddered to a halt. They were still half a klick or more from their destination in the far Northwest, almost to the Maryland line, a few blocks west of the boundary of Rock Creek Park, but it was part of the agreement that Mobile One would not itself put in an appearance at the Rubble Mart. It was felt its awesome armament might tend to overshadow the proceedings. As a matter of fact, it was the Guardians' intention to overshadow the proceedings, but Rogers and Sloan insisted this had to be played subtly.

McKay, Sloan, and Tom Rogers dismounted into the dust that covered the street. A moment later Eli Scott joined them, straightening his tie. Each man checked his weapons. Scott had a mini-Uzi in a shoulder holster under his coat. Rogers had a Smith and Wesson 3000 pump shotgun, Sloan his usual Galil-203 combo. Billy McKay had a standard Uzi. He was giving his MP-5 a rest—it was a specialist's gun, not meant for out-and-out firefights. And if the discussion turned to busting caps, silence would be the last thing that mattered. He kind of wanted his M-60, but judged it was a little inappropriate for formal occasions.

There'd been no question of them going unarmed. Casey Wilson had suggested that be a term of the conference, that everyone should show up onsite without weapons. It had been hooted down. Tom explained gently that indiges—indigenous forces—never, never went anywhere without their guns. They were a cross between a phallic symbol and a security blanket—and, no less here in the ruins of what had been a nation's capital than in the Third World jungles where Rogers had spent most of his professional life, an indispensable tool of survival. As a matter of fact, the Guardians hadn't even been able to talk the conferees into accepting a ban on automatic weapons.

Sloan frowned at his leader. "You're taking a shovel to the conference?" he asked in disbelief.

"It's an entrenching tool." McKay slapped the haft of the half-meter implement slung at his belt. "Come in handy when the bullshit gets so deep we have to dig to breathe."

Before Sloan could dream up a response McKay turned. "Right, Case, you get Mobile One squared away out of sight somewhere, then follow along and take up position somewhere you can follow us if you need to boogie in a hurry."

"Right, Billy, I know that."

And why am I babbling shit everybody already knows? He squinted up into the diffuse brightness of the sky. "Let's go." He started to shut the side hatch.

"Billy," Casey said softly, "it's a trap, isn't it?"

"Shit yes," McKay said. "But it's okay. We got 'em surrounded." He slammed shut the steel door.

The V-450 backed up with a squealing and grumbling of rubble, chugged away down a side street. The party set off walking, weapons ready. Any trouble now would likely be no more than a random ambush; if, as each man suspected in his gut, the shithammer was about to come down for true, it would do so at the meeting. But they couldn't be too careful.

They inclined north and west, and in a few blocks were hailed by a man with a single feather stuck into the headband tied around his temples. As expected. Eli Scott stepped forward as the rest of the Tide Camp contingent emerged from cover to greet them. He'd accompanied the Guardians to this rendezvous in hopes of helping forestall any "accidents" on the part of disgruntled warriors. Even though Soong had spoken, a lot of them still hadn't forgotten what happened at the Lincoln Memorial.

The big man himself appeared, stepping over a line of debris that had been a wall. He was dressed in plain army olive drab fatigues this morning, without rank badges, and looked like nothing so much as Mao Zedong ready to set off on the Long March. And trotting at his heels came his very own Colonel Callan, Andy Aramyan, wearing of all the damn things a pale blue shirt and a tie and a blue blazer buttoned up the front.

"Check it out," McKay said. "You going to a wedding?"

Andy scowled. "Or a funeral, maybe." He had his pet weapon along, an old AKM he'd carried in the field. It went peculiarly with the blazer.

There were about a dozen more of the Tide Camp warriors in their exotic plumage. The Guardians recognized the lean long frame and bleached hair of Tyler, and the rest of the patrol that accompanied them on the rescue mission as well, Martin with his necklace of fingerbones and cat skull, Rosen intense in his mime's makeup, Harris and Langetti, big blond Kerry, one eye socket still faintly outlined in smudgy green from where McKay had hit him.

And here was McKay's old marine buddy, Bill Madden, last seen in the mob getting ready to incinerate Uhuru Assad, back in his ODs and reluctant to look McKay in the eye. With them came a handful of others whose names nobody knew, and who eyed the Guardians with a flatness that verged on outright hostility.

"Can we trust these people?" asked Sam Sloan, speaking for the benefit of the communicators alone, not for the first time.

"Who the hell knows? I can sure throw good buddy Andy a lot farther than I'd ever trust him, that's for sure."

"Do we got a choice?"

"No."

They set off north in a vee formation, Martin swinging in the lead with his M-203 and the rest of the Tide Camp troopees trailing back along what they estimated were both sides of the street. The Guardians walked inside the vee with Soong and Aramyan and Scott, making it tricky to backshoot them. The Tide Camp fighters, as usual, bristled weapons; but Soong was unarmed.

They marched several hundred meters, through a trendy commercial district with more than a feel of the suburbs to it. There had been a lot of fires here, but the blast damage was minimal.

Abruptly things widened out into an entire hectare, it seemed, of parking lot, miraculously all but devoid of derelict cars. In the middle of it humped a once-landscaped low mound of hill, from which rose the sporadically charred gray walls of what looked for all the world like an Italian Renaissance city in miniature.

It was going to be the Villa Firenze, Washington's biggest shopping mall. It had cost a whole boatload of money to buy the land, which didn't exactly come cheap inside the Beltway, and taken years to straighten out the zoning hassles; one consortium had gone broke trying to build it, and the one that took over after receivership had just gotten the thing finished and mostly occupied and were getting ready for the grand opening when they held the One-Day War instead. Which was why no cars. But the vast black expanse of asphalt wasn't unoccupied.

A crude three-strand barbed-wire fence had been strung around the perimeter. It was a pretty wobbly structure, but its purpose was mostly symbolic. There was a gate of meter-high barbed-wire coils, which a couple of burly dudes with blue armbands and M-16s obligingly hooked aside for the party. Soong, Andy, and Eli Scott moved to the front with the Guardians. They saluted, which the guards made an earnest effort at returning, and then marched in through the wire while the rest of the squad fell in behind.

"Welcome to Rubble Mart," said the taller guard, a burly young man with curly black hair and beard, apparently out of habit.

Only a few of the packing-crate stalls and scavenged tables were occupied today; for once in a great long while, there would be little business as usual at the Rubble Mart.

"How very curious," Soong murmured from the side

of his mouth to McKay and Sloan as they walked toward the little town on its green island. He had never been here before.

"This is nothing, Captain," Sloan assured him.

He and McKay had been here a couple of days before when the mart was in its glory. It was quite the spectacle. A flea market of the damned.

There was plenty of stuff to be had—scarf—from the ruins. But what you needed or wanted wasn't necessarily what was to be had in your territory. Nor even necessarily in your neighbor's, so that raiding or pushing rivals off their hunting grounds might not fill the bill.

Thus trade. Even in the corpse of a dead city, one of the oldest of human instincts came to the fore. If there was something you lacked, this was where you came to look for it; if there was something you wanted to unload, this was the place to do it.

On the Guardians' first visit, they'd passed displays of just about anything portable you could imagine and then some. There was canned food and candy and sacks of flour, mostly full of worms (a good source of protein). There were huge black velvet paintings of tigers and Elvis and Jesus. Table lamps in exotic shapes there was no current to run, kerosene lamps and the fuel to burn in them; tools, birdcages, stuffed toys; swimsuits, tuxedos, and army jackets; fresh produce; overstuffed chairs with watermarked upholstery; crates of books and magazines and writing paper, not much in demand but commanding a high price from those who wanted it; broken clocks; a couple of sinks; blenders and a washing machine and VCRs and televisions and computers, some obviously broken, none of which would run until a power station came back online; fresh batteries (a premium item); records, sunglasses, suntan oil, axe handles; a pig; candles, sheepskin car-seat covers, boxes full of trash. A skinny teenaged girl with paper-white skin and sunken eyes, and a discreet little pup tent set up for the privacy-minded. Cigarettes. Bicycles. In short, almost anything, from the vital to the ludicrous.

One thing had been conspicuously lacking: weapons, except for a few displays of cheap pocket knives and some pistols that looked as if they'd been dredged out of the river. Those were top-price items, like gasoline, quality booze, and drugs both pharmaceutical and recreational; those tended to be vended in the more exclusive—and secure—confines of the shopping center itself. But just about everything else under the sun was spread out here under the sun, day by day.

It was all owned and operated by a squat little character named Kostakis and his extended family. They'd moved back in as soon as the fallout had died back to the point it would no longer make your balls glow blue and keep you awake at night. They would buy and sell stuff themselves, or rent spaces to anyone who wished to do so. And they had done well.

McKay and Rogers had seen it before. Even in the wreckage of West Beirut, battered to rubble and patrolled by armed men of half a dozen nations and who knew how many factions, with all normal routes of trade and distribution thoroughly blocked, and with every chieftain and warlord trying to impose his own scheme of rationing, markets had sprung up. You couldn't stop them, and when no one was trying they could be quite lucrative.

And Rubble Mart was neutral ground, the only such patch in the District of Columbia. That was a major reason the Guardians had picked it. Hereabouts a Blood could rub elbows with a Rebel Runner, a Warlord with a Death Commando, if not in amity, then generally without violence. The peace was enforced by members of the

Kostakis clan and their various hirelings, but more by the pressure of custom. People had learned the hard way that they needed the mart.

In the lean cold times of winter there had been some raids, culminating in a bloody shoot-out. The Kostakis had shut the place down and retreated to the villa. And in six weeks the head of the last man responsible for the attack was delivered to them. Rubble Mart was a necessity.

All of which would slow down the Guardians' dear friend Ivan Vesensky for less than the time it would take him to blink. He didn't have to live here, after all, and the type of people he was pitching his appeal to weren't the sort who generally bothered sorting out the consequences of their actions, at least not when emotion or desire urged them to those actions. Mainly the place had been picked in hopes the habit of neutrality would keep some of the Guardians' allies from eating one another.

The mall itself was larger than it looked at first glance, better than a hundred meters to a side. Walkways curved up from the parking lot to a terrace, on which their host himself awaited them, his forehead bright and mustache heavy with sweat. "Welcome, gentlemen," he said as they approached. "The others have already begun to arrive."

He led them into the complex itself. Little narrow streets wound around narrow structures two and three stories in height. "You could just about get lost in here," Sloan commented. It had been cunningly laid out to give the illusion of being larger than it was.

In the center of it all was a tiny flagstone plaza, with a dry fountain in the middle of it. The meeting room was in the main dining room on the ground floor of a cafeteria that fronted the plaza.

They thanked Mr. Kostakis, who bowed formally and

hurried off to await more conferees. Soong dismissed his escort to wander around the complex, then went into the building with Andy, Madden, and Eli Scott. McKay looked to the other Guardians.

"Well," he said, "here goes nothing."

"The reason I choose to retain my 'slave name' as you choose to call it," Josephus McDaniels said frostily, "is that it seems peculiar to foresake the name of the family that freed my ancestor from slavery a year before the Civil War in favor of a name borrowed from the Arabs who sold *his* ancestors into slavery. And need I remind you, Mr. Jabbar, that our roots lie in a culture that itself practiced slavery?"

Malcolm Jabbar stared through slits at the huge man who sat across the long table from him. Sitting several seats down, McKay took a swig of tepid canned beer, sighed, and checked his watch. *Almost 1200, and we still ain't talked about anything that means anything.* A swig. *Hell, a quarter of the people ain't even showed yet.*

Sloan grinned at him across the table. "How do you like playing Talleyrand, McKay?"

McKay glared at him and wished you could tell somebody to fuck off at a summit meeting.

Even without the full contingent there must have been forty people in the room. Almost twenty groups were represented so far. Their dress ranged from rags to the scrubbed-farmer look affected by McDaniels and his people to the immaculately tailored Jabbar. The Bloods were there, looking flash, and the Rangers and the Super Machos—predominantly Puerto Rican groups, and mortal enemies until now—the Georgetown Boys, the Rats, and Warlords, the boss of the Nuclear Winners with blue-dyed hair standing straight up from her skull. The Tide Camp representatives in the room were pretty somberly dressed, but the wildest of their warriors circulating outside would have fit right into this crew.

Several teenagers, apparently more of Kostakis's clansfolk, circulated through the crowd, distributing drinks from carts and various canned munchies. The whole show reminded McKay a lot of the parties he'd gone to as a high school student back in Pittsburgh, except nobody'd thrown up and there'd only been one fight so far. Unlike the old days, he wasn't hoping for more.

He looked around. McDaniels had gotten sidetracked into an intense discussion with some young Hispanic woman. Tom Rogers was over at a booth by the wall trying to convince a couple of dudes from rival gangs not to puncture each other, at least not in here. Surreptitiously, McKay checked his watch again.

Oh well. At least we're still alive.

When she couldn't take it anymore, Uhuru Assad stood and walked to the door of her cell. It was filled with that total darkness you only find in an interior room, but she'd paced it often enough during the caged-animal phase of her captivity. She found the light, flipped it on. She had no idea what time it was, only that she'd come to a decision which would probably cost her a lot of her self-esteem and, possibly, her life.

Tom, she thought. She was about to turn on the only man she'd ever thought she loved. But she could not let Tom Rogers die. He had given her more than just her life. He had given her respect.

She reached a hand, touched the door. The metal was cool to her fingertips. *What if they've got those crazies from Tide Camp guarding the hallways? They'll take me, they'll hurt me, they'll burn me!*

She turned and slumped with her back to the door until she fought the panic down. *Take it easy. You're a big girl now.* She almost laughed. She was all of nineteen years old, and was just shutting out her first career as agitator, terrorist, big-time revolutionary leader.

With sudden resolution she turned, pounded with one fist on the door. "Hello? Is anybody out there?"

No answer.

For a moment she just knew the hallway outside was filled with painted warriors, stalking up and down wondering which locked door concealed their quarry from them, knew that they would break it down and rush in and take her and make her scream. But nothing happened. She hit the door again, called louder. No result. Finally she shrugged and tried the knob.

The door opened.

"I'll be damned," she said.

Tentatively she stepped out into the hall. The glow from the overhead fluorescents gave no clue to the time of day. *Mr. Tom motherfucking Rogers, you did this. Why?* She shook her head. That dude played games within games. And yet he had been square with her, more square than any man she'd ever met.

And then she knew why he had done it. *Calculated risk.* Well, she'd show him how his calculations turned out. She ran down the hall toward the stairs.

Rogers sidled up to McKay, who was trying not to slump under the table. "Looks like this is all we're going to get, Billy. Shall we call this meeting to order?"

McKay choked back a yawn. "Roger that."

He caught Sloan's eye, nodded. Sloan cleared his throat audibly. "Ladies and gentlemen." He ignored the ripple of laughter that circled the room. "The time has come to begin discussing our mutual problem.''

"I thought that's what we'd been doing," a Hispanic voice remarked.

Gosh, this is fun, McKay thought. He glanced up to see Jabbar hovering next to him.

"Pardon me, Lieutenant McKay, would you be so kind as to tell me the time? My watch seems to have stopped," Jabbar said.

McKay raised an eyebrow. Jabbar struck him as the type to brush each tooth individually; surprising he'd let the thing run down. He checked his own timepiece, told the man without consciously registering the hour.

"Thank you. If you'll excuse me momentarily, I'd best go check on my men." McKay frowned slightly as he watched the small man walk toward the front door. There was something here not quite right, but he couldn't put his finger on it.

Jeffrey MacGregor sat at the desk he'd had moved into the Lincoln Suite and thumbed through yet another sheaf of computer printouts. *As if it matters,* he told himself bitterly. He fought the urge to jump up for the hundredth time and pace over to the Rose Room to stare north across the ruins to where, perhaps, the fate of the country itself was being discussed. It seemed absurd that a convocation of squatters and youth gangs should be so momentous.

But if the Guardians pull this off—if they survive—then we might really be able to get back to work.

He sighed, sipped from a glass of tea with a sprig of mint placed in it by one of the ever-helpful Tide Camp people who'd volunteered as servants. He frowned at the paper, as if trying to squeeze some significance from it.

"Mr. President?" a voice said behind him.

His head snapped up, around. A young black woman with short hair, dressed in jeans and a man's shirt, stood in the open doorway. "Mr. President, I'm Uhuru Assad. I need your help. The lives of the Guardians depend on it."

Malcolm Jabbar's hand was in his pocket as the front door of the restaurant swung to behind him. The early afternoon sunlight was warm on his face and hands, and he felt warmth answering within. This was it. The proverbial moment he'd been waiting for.

He pulled a small black plastic object about the size and shape of a *Star Trek* communicator from his pocket, flipped it open. On it was a numeric keypad. He punched a brief combination. All but the last number —he didn't know whether there was enough room in the little remote actuator to hold a plastic explosive charge large enough to kill him, nor did he have reason to believe Ian Victor wanted to do so. But just in case, he would wait until he was safely inside a building in the next miniature block, and then let his assistant who awaited him there key in the final digit.

No point in taking unnecessary chances when mastery of the ruins lay—literally—within his grasp.

The door had just swung shut behind Jabbar when a female voice shrilled in the Guardians' ears, "Tom! Tom, are you there? You're in a trap! *Jabbar is one of them!*"

CHAPTER
EIGHTEEN ——————

All the tumblers clicked inside McKay's skull. He knew why Jabbar had excused himself. He flashed to his feet. "Out!" he roared. "Everybody get out of this room, right now. There's a bomb in here!"

The room was full of eyes set in blank faces. The serving kids had all evaporated—forewarned, of course. McKay grabbed handfuls of the two people nearest him and raced for the nearest exit, the passageway behind him leading to the kitchen. Instinct told him they would only have mined the meeting chamber, and if his guess was wrong that was it for him.

Soong reacted a millisecond later, at the same time the other two Guardians did, like McKay grabbing whoever was nearest him and thrusting them toward the door. Tom Rogers picked up a chair and hurled it through windows, miraculously intact until now, whose lower halves were fake stained glass; there was no way everyone was going to get out the few doors in time.

Sloan followed his example, and both men dived out into the street.

There was no way everyone was going to get out period.

McKay hit the swinging doors at the other end of the passage and slammed them open. He stepped to one side, while frantic conferees streamed past. Against all training, experience, and common sense, he poked his head back round the corner of the door.

Josephus McDaniels stood at the other end of the short corridor, his long arms scooping in people and hurling them down it like sacks of grain. Abruptly the huge man was silhouetted in a blinding blue-white flash, and forever after Mckay believed he saw the man's outline begin to fray, even though he knew his eyes could not register anything happening that quickly. McKay jerked back as a wave of debris, including what a second before had been McDaniels, blasted into the kitchen.

There hadn't been just one bomb. Ivan Vesensky was more than just figuratively a demolitions expert. With some help from Jabbar's more advanced terrorists, he had wired up the booths, the brass-finished pillars that held up the tables, strategic light fixtures—a score of charges cunningly emplaced to turn the conference room into a slaughterhouse. As far as half the delegates went, he succeeded.

Had it not been for the defection of Malcolm Jabbar's former lover, he would have made a clean sweep.

For one of the few times in his life, Malcolm Jabbar grinned when he heard the blast. His public persona was such that he displayed anger more readily than any other emotion. It reflected his private personality. But now he grinned.

Ian Victor definitely has his uses, he told himself. *I hope it won't be necessary to dispose of him too soon.* Nodding to his subordinate, who stood by with the detonator in his hand and one finger still on the key pad, he walked out into the street to take a look at his triumph.

The street in front of the restaurant was full of broken glass and milling bodies. That didn't alarm him. The explosion was the signal for his own men and the horde the "Witch King" had hidden inside the mall, to pour out and massacre the retinues of the conference attendees killed by the blast.

Then he saw that two of the people up the block were wearing coveralls of a distinctive silver-gray color, and belatedly realized that something was very, very wrong.

Very deliberately Tom Rogers raised his Galil SAR to his shoulder, while Jabbar watched as if mesmerized. He saw an ejaculation of flame, and the burst that hit him felt like a single massive impact against the front of his body. Then he hit the pavement as if he was landing all but weightless on a fine feather mattress, and lay there looking up past the gray buildings that seemed to lean together at the featureless white sky. And then he died.

McKay pushed out the back door of the restaurant at the same time a whole crowd of people tried to barge in. For a moment he stood just outside the door, surrounded by a lot of dudes in rags and spikes and warpaint. Then a shot cracked off almost in his face, he felt the hot breath of muzzle blast, and a bullet flaked off a patch of stucco to his right; and then lots of things began to happen.

There was no time to get at the Uzi slung over his back. His hand dropped to his belt, closed around the wood haft of the entrenching tool Sloan had been riding him about. He yanked it free. It wasn't one of your cheap U.S.-issue E-tools with the folding heads that busted right off. It was Swiss, one piece, a good steel head trimly fastened to a hardwood haft. Implements just like it, their heads likewise honed to razor sharpness, had been very popular weapons in the trenches in World War One.

McKay raised the tool, struck. A pale contorted face before him split like a cantaloupe. The kid went down with his brains spilling out over his nose as McKay wrenched the weapon free and slammed it into the shoulder of a burly dude with a two-tone Mohawk, almost severing the arm. A third attacker, more alert, danced back, and the backhand sweep of the shovel ended in the chest of a very surprised fourth one. His eyes got big, blood geysered out around the blade, and he crumpled.

Unfortunately the blade was wedged between his ribs. McKay bent with him, trying to wrench his weapon free. Somebody lunged for him. He smashed his left fist into the guy's face, felt him fall back. Then they were swarming all over him, getting in one another's way in their eagerness.

McKay released the shovel's handle. Kicking savagely, scything left and right with his elbows, he backed his attackers off for the split second needed to pluck a fragmentation grenade from his belt. There was a game his daddy had told him about that the marines played in Nam, back in the Hill Fights before Khe Sanh. He pulled the pin—

—and let the grenade fall at his feet.

His attackers froze. "Grenade!" screeched one with a fine grasp of the obvious.

McKay dropped flat onto the cement, banging his

knee and his cheek and burying his face in his hands. He was betting on his Kevlar body armor and the tendency of grenade blasts to propagate upwards, away from the ground. It was a long way from a sure bet. That's what made it fun.

The grenade went. McKay felt stinging in his right biceps and thighs and a god-almighty kick in the ribs. He let adrenaline snap him to his feet as though there were a long elastic band attached to his shoulders that stretched right on up into heaven.

It was very satisfactory; bodies everywhere. He unslung his Uzi, held it one-handed, stuck his head back in the door. "Haul ass," he bellowed at the handful of survivors huddled in the kitchen. They streamed past him into the street, skidding a little on spilled blood and assorted organic matter. McKay leaned back against the doorjamb for just a fraction of a second, squeezed his eyes shut and shook his head. Then he stooped, recovered his E-tool with a wrench of his shoulders, and ran around the building to rejoin his comrades.

The street in front of the restaurant was momentarily clear. At either end of the block Sam Sloan could see confused melees as ambushers battled with fighters from half a dozen factions of the fledgling alliance. People were screaming and moaning all around him. From the swirling blackness in the restaurant came no sounds at all.

"Casey," he panted, "call in the mortar."

"Can't, Sam," returned Casey, who was remotely patched through Mobile One to the radio operators in Tide Camp. "The four-deuce's knocked out. Got rocketed about the time you reported the blast there, and the eighty-one mike-mike is out of range."

"Shit." They were on the receiving end of a well-timed and well-laid trap. *As if we didn't know.*

Bullets spattered the restaurant's facade. Soong, who'd made it to safety with both Scott and Aramyan, grunted and sagged back against the building. Sloan pivoted and fired the 203. The white phosphorus grenade barely had time to arm itself before popping in the third-story window across the street from which the gunfire had come.

The explosion blasted the sniper out the window. He fell to the street in a fall of fairy-dust glitter. Except the sparkling dust was phosphorus fragments that burned at a temperature that would melt steel. He landed on the street and writhed and screamed as tentacles of white smoke waved about him.

McKay came pelting up with several survivors in tow and Sloan recoiled. The big ex-marine looked ghastly, face blackened and bloody, coveralls charred and ripped and soaked with the blood of friend and enemy alike.

"Where's Bill Madden?" McKay grunted.

"He didn't make it," Scott said, holding his mini-Uzi muzzle-up and ready. "Didn't even try. He and Andy pushed Soong outside, then Bill went back to help the rest."

McKay spit out bloody grit. "Shit."

Soong was leaning against the wall with blood squeezing out between fingers he held pressed to his side, trying to fend off Andy Aramyan. "I'm fine, don't worry about me," he kept saying.

"You stupid fuck! Look what you did!" Andy shrieked at McKay. "He's hit. Do you see that? He's hit!" Tears streamed from his dark eyes, blood from his right ear.

For a moment Sloan thought McKay would shoot Andy, but instead McKay turned abruptly and hosed a long burst at the attackers who were suddenly bearing down on them across the little square.

Andy, his Kalashnikov gone with the wind, ripped his Redhawk from its holster and fired. The slug caught a man who was bounding through the defunct fountain in mid-stride and threw him back down among the lime flakes.

Sloan yanked the breech of the 203 shut on a multiple-projectile round and fired. The charge whistled into the faces of the wave of attackers, rolling several of them on the pavement. The rest faltered, turned, ran.

"This ain't gonna last," McKay shouted. "Tom, lead off."

Rogers didn't have to ask where to. Any direction was as good—or as bad—as another, as long as they came out on the south side where Casey could give them a modicum of covering fire. Rogers headed straight off along the block, past the sprawled bodies of Jabbar and his subordinate, who'd made the mistake of running out to his leader's aid. As they passed, Soong shrugged off Scott and Andy, who were trying to help him walk, and stooped to recover the man's fallen M-16.

Ahead the street was blocked by men and women battling hand to hand with fists, knives, gun butts, makeshift clubs. Rogers threw a tear gas grenade into the midst of it all. The battle began to break up in choking, hacking clumps.

Tom blitzed on without bothering to pull on his gas mask. The others followed. The Guardians and the Tide Camp people could handle CS in brief exposure; the others would be okay if they had the sense just to cruise on in a straight line, and that was the best deal anyone was going to offer them.

They stumbled into the stinging smoke, a Super Macho and a Warlord supporting one another, McDaniels' aide weeping without any help from the tear gas, McKay splitting heads with his Swiss shovel, Nova of the Winners blazing away with a Bren 10-mm in her left hand—even though a jagged end of her broken right humerus was sticking out through her bare biceps—a handful of others.

Shouts, screams, gasps, and they were through. Fortunately for them the narrow streets of the mall wound crookedly in and around. Enemies they encountered generally didn't get a shot at them until they were at close quarters, and then the heavy firepower of the Guardians and the Tide Camp men mowed them down.

On the run they picked up other survivors, people who had escorted their leaders to the meeting and then been turned loose to wander the complex. From a street to the left spilled a half-dozen armed, painted men. McKay swung his Uzi to cover them, froze his trigger finger just in time. It was Tyler and some of the Tidal contingent. McKay nodded to them and ran on.

Ahead of them the street spilled out into the broader boulevard that led out of the complex. Pounding on point McKay could see a number of the opposition, some Jabbar's natty blacks, others as outlandishly clad as the Tide Camp warriors, standing around the intersection wondering where the action was. Shots and shouts were pressing the fugitives close from behind; the action was just about to find the boys ahead. Sam Sloan fired a white phosphorus grenade to clear the way, and they charged out of the side street into the smoke.

McKay ran smack into someone, smashed the Uzi into his face. The man fell, tried to struggle to his feet, only to have Aramyan stick his horse pistol into his face and blow the side of his head off. The main entrance was thirty meters ahead. McKay raced for it, spraying bullets at the handful of black leather boys who stood just inside it.

Kerry loped at Soong's side, weeping with concern. "Chief, let me help you—"

A bullet caught him low in the back. He sobbed once, seized Soong's arm convulsively, dropped to his knees, toppled to the side. Soong shook his huge head sadly, fired a burst behind him, and ran on.

The mob was right behind them now. It overran a pair of stragglers, literally tore them apart with knives and spikes. Sam Sloan turned back, dropped to one knee, sprayed the onrushing mass with full-auto fire.

"Sam, come on!" yelled Tom Rogers.

"We'll never outrun them like this. Go on, I'll hold 'em."

A hand twisted in his collar, hauled him to his feet. Andy Aramyan was glaring up at him with hot black eyes. "You run, fancy soldier. Run all the way back to your President. I stop them."

"Come on, Sam," Rogers urged.

Sam and the Armenian were now tail-end Charlies, the mob barely ten meters away. Sam ran for the exit.

Andy Aramyan stepped into the middle of the street, arms outstretched. His coat was torn, one sleeve gone, his tie askew. He was unarmed. The frontrunning pursuers slowed, eyeing him suspiciously.

"Grab him," a voice shouted from behind them. "Take him alive. We can have some fun."

Leather kids surrounded him, laughing, plucking at his clothes. "You're gonna beg us for death, brother," they shouted as they laid hands upon him.

Andy smiled beatifically. "Not when I've got it in my hand," he said. "So long, suckers."

The device he held in his right hand said *clack*.

The Claymore strapped to his chest beneath his shirt swept the street clean of life in a flash and a doomsday roar.

• • •

Inaccurately aimed fire cracked after the fugitives from the upper floors of the shopping mall as they poured down the brief green slope like a flash flood. They were well out into the parking lot, dodging tables and booths, when the first pursuer popped out of the entryway through which they'd fled. He took four steps before Casey's bullet, fired from a kilometer away, hit him in the sternum and dropped him.

"Casey, pull back," ordered McKay, not realizing the fourth Guardian had opened fire. "Bring Mobile One, and for God's sake hurry."

"Roger, Billy." But Casey didn't react at once. A very interesting target had caught his eye as he scanned his high-tech electronic sight back and forth over his side of the mall.

A loggia ran around the top story of the building nearest him, and on it appeared a black-and-silver figure with an elaborately made-up face. It leaped up onto the guardrail, held to a pillar with one hand while the other waved what appeared to be a samurai *katana*, apparently to rally the forces belatedly spilling out of the complex.

Casey settled the long barrel of the rifle a little more firmly into the sandbag he carried with him for the purpose. Even for the exquisitely tuned M-40X sniper's weapon with its cutting-edge computerized scope it was a long shot. The first man he'd dropped had had the misfortune of running into a shot prepared for hours ago; Casey knew where the pursuit would be coming out, and was ready for it. He didn't have all the time in the world for this shot.

Who the target was he didn't know. If he was lucky, it would be the Witch King—whom he hoped was their old enemy Vesensky. He didn't permit himself to speculate.

He just knew the outlandish apparition was helping direct the pursuit. That was all he needed to know.

Coolly he centered his sight picture on the man on the railing, touched a button on the side of the sight until glowing bars at the top and bottom of his field of vision had moved to mark the upper extent of his target's white rat's-nest hair and the high heels of his boots. He lined up the glowing crosshair with the center of the black leather straps crossing the chest, took a breath, let some of it out, caught it, squeezed.

The Witch King swept his sword down in a sweeping gesture to point after the fleeing party. Halfway down a 7.62-mm bullet caught it and snapped it off a foot from the hand guard. Deflected a couple of degrees from its course, the bullet punched through the right side of Ivan Vesensky's chest, twisting his body so that he lost his grip on the pillar and pitched forward onto the grassy slope.

A thousand meters away, Casey watched him fall. He took no satisfaction from the deed, merely waited until the body hit turf, then stood, recovered his sandbag, and rapidly pulled out.

Running at McKay's side, Eli Scott uttered a soft grunt, fell down and rolled over and over on the asphalt. McKay glanced back. Aramyan's sacrifice had won them a respite, enough to see them three-quarters of the way across the parking lot. But now it was over.

Sloan turned back, fired a grenade. It landed beside the stream of howling figures rushing out from the complex. They saw several go down, but the rest came on.

Nova of the Nuclear Winners staggered by, barely keeping her feet. She'd lost a lot of blood. McKay caught her good arm, whose hand still clutched her empty pistol, wrapped it around his neck. She would

slow him down. But what the hell? They weren't going
to make it anyway.

"Hold on, Lieutenant McKay," whispered a faraway
voice in his ear. "Relief party is on its way."

McKay looked out the window. It wasn't worth the
trouble to respond. By the time the trucks carrying the
Tide Camp reinforcements could crawl across the intervening kilometers of rubble the bad guys would have
finished skinning them.

A dozen of them had made it to the doubtful shelter
of this three-story office building, standing alone on a
mostly trashed-out block. The three Guardians, Soong,
Nova, Tyler and Martin, a few others. Thin-faced
Rosen, who always covered his face in white pancake
makeup and insisted on the warrior's prerogative, had
sucked a round in the leg a couple of blocks ago. The
pursuers caught him, smashed his head with a piece of
masonry. At least it had been quick. McKay wasn't sure
the rest of them would be that lucky.

From somewhere on the other side of the building
came the thump of Sloan's grenade launcher. He and
Martin were down to a handful of grenades each. The
defenders were reduced to firing single rounds, trying to
conserve their dwindling ammo for the big push the
enemy was preparing. For a moment, McKay wondered
why. Unless maybe it was to have fireworks to mark
their passing.

Fuck that, he thought savagely. He'd save his bullets
until he had good targets for them. And when they'd
found good homes, he'd fight with his pistol, and when
that ran dry with his E-tool and his knife and when
those were broken he'd use his hands and feet, and
when they were gone, he'd bite the bastards, like the guy
in the old Monty Python flick. He was William God-

damn Kosciusko McKay, and he wouldn't quit fighting until he was dead at the earliest.

"Here they come, Billy," Rogers said. The enemy wasn't playing this with much finesse. They didn't have to. They had their quarry surrounded, and they had at least a ten-to-one advantage. They just came on as if they'd never stop.

Sam Sloan kissed his last grenade good-bye. It popped practically at the base of their stronghold. The phosphorus clawed enemies down shrieking. The rest didn't even hesitate. They smelled blood. In seconds they would fill this whole building like gas squirted from high pressure tanks.

Then thunder rumbled on the south. Spiked warriors racing to the entry on Sam's side of the building suddenly went tumbling down the block like tumbleweeds blown by the wind. Sam frowned, lowered his rifle a hair. He couldn't make this out at all.

Again thunder. More attackers fell, and those still erect began to stumble to a halt and stare wildly around. Then a new roaring, rhythmic, higher-pitched and louder than the first, and a line of explosions shattered a storefront to Sam's left.

"What the fuck is that?" McKay's voice asked.

Sam did a very foolish thing. He stood up, stuck his head out the window and craned his neck to peer up the street. It didn't matter; by that point all the attackers with legs still under them were using them to go elsewhere at a high rate of speed. Because chugging down the street like a pissed-off dinosaur came Mobile One its own self, and its turret was spouting flame to put a dragon to shame.

Cheers broke out behind Sloan. "Look at those bastards run!"

"It's the cavalry, Billy," Sam said, "Just in time."

"If that's Casey driving that thing, then who the hell is shooting?"

"Are you complaining?"

The armored car pulled to a stop right under Sam's window and idled, its engine grumbling contentedly. The other Guardians came out to meet it. The driver's top hatch popped open and Casey stuck his head out. "You guys all right?"

The three looked at one another. They were bloody, burned, battered, and dirty. Sloan had a flesh wound through his upper thigh—a 5.56, missed bone and artery, hadn't tumbled, so it wasn't bad.

"Yeah, Case," he said, "We're doing just fine."

"So who the hell's the gunner?" McKay demanded.

In response the turret hatch opened and out popped the head and shoulders of Marshal Commander Uhuru Assad, late of the BLA. "Hi."

"I'll be dipped in shit," McKay said.

"After she called in the warning that it was a trap, she, like, borrowed a motorcycle from the White House garage," Casey explained. "She headed up this way to see if she could lend a hand."

"Unarmed?" Sloan asked. He sounded impressed.

She shrugged. "Reckoned I'd work something out. Anyway, I ran into Casey and the behemoth here." She patted the top of the turret. "So everything came out all right."

"I took a moment to show her the layout of the turret controls. She's not, like, as good as you, Sam, but she did all right, didn't she?"

"I'll be dipped in shit," McKay repeated.

"Probably," Sam Sloan agreed.

EPILOGUE

The fledgling alliance had suffered a terrible blow. But their enemies got the worst of it. Jabbar and Vesensky had bet everything on a one-shot bid for victory.

They lost.

Within minutes after Mobile One relieved the refugees forted up in their lone building, reinforcements began pouring into the area, not just from Tide Camp but from the other parties to the alliance, alerted by radio to Jabbar's treachery. It was the turn of the Witch King's subjects to be hunted through the rubble. Not many of them escaped.

The Guardians handed the injured Soong over to his people. Then, leaving the mopping-up to their enthusiastic allies, they took a squad of Tidal warriors to call on Seth Rushton on Capitol Hill. They were very interested in finding out why he had been conveniently absent from the doomed summit.

They got their answer—as far as they could know —when they came under fire from Jabbar's gunmen, left behind to guard the American Union captives. The Guardians were not in an accommodating mood. The very fact that they were alive signified to Jabbar's heavies that their leader almost certainly wasn't. Any idea of a bitter-end resistance evaporated before the ferocity of the Guardians' assault; almost immediately the defenders were throwing their arms away, trying to surrender.

Some of them even got to.

Bemused, the Guardians watched a tearful reunion between Rushton and his wife. "Oh, darling," she cried, throwing herself sobbing at his neck. "You don't know how frightened I was. What I did, I did to save your life."

Rushton patted her back and mumbled encouragements. "Sure. Sure, I understand."

"And if you believe that," McKay said under his breath, "I got a bridge for you." He scowled, lit a cigar, just praying the skinny little son of a bitch would tell him he couldn't smoke in the Rotunda.

"We got what we needed, Mr. Soong," Sam Sloan explained in the cool dimness of the Tide Camp's chieftain's hut. "The fight pulled the various factions of our alliance together. Our mission's accomplished. The capital is secured."

"Not without cost." Heavy-lidded eyes glistened.

"Aramyan saved us," rasped McKay as if the words hurt him, which they did. "We'd never have made it without him."

Soong nodded. "Nor would we without you"—he nodded at each of the Guardians in turn—"or this brave young woman here."

Uhuru Assad smiled and put her arm around Tom's waist.

"Or yourself, sir," Sloan said. "Or Scott, or Madden, or Kerry, Tyler and the rest."

"Yeah, well, we're all a bunch of heroes," said McKay, who was beginning to get embarrassed.

"Indubitably," Soong said. "And what will you gentlemen do now?"

"Go back to piecing together the Blueprint, I guess, man," Casey said.

"Don't forget we've got to retrieve the Blueprint personnel from Luxor," Sloan said.

McKay grinned a lopsided grin. "Yeah," he said, "and if you think the Witch King was bad, just wait until Marguerite Connoly moves in and takes over."

Soong cocked his vast head to one side, puzzled.

"It'll be a relief to get out of this rubble and into the countryside again," Sloan said. "I can barely remember what green looks like."

"And what of your enemy Vesensky?"

"Casey's description of the man he shot matches the way our prisoners describe the Witch King." He grinned. "Looks as if we've finally put *paid* to old Ivan's account."

McKay scowled. "Don't be so sure of that. We never found no body."

"When Casey shoots somebody, he stays down," Sloan replied blithely. He clapped his leader on the arm. "C'mon, McKay, lighten up. We won."

McKay took his unlit cigar from his mouth, studied it as if not sure how it got there. "Yeah," he said at last, "yeah, I guess we did."

"*Wer da?*" challenged a soldier with the blue badge of the FSE on the shoulder of his *Bundeswehr* uniform.

The other members of the patrol melted into cover beside the road on the outskirts of Baltimore. A figure tottered out of the dawn mist. "*Mein Gott*," the soldier breathed.

It was a wild-haired apparition, its face smeared in red and black, clad in shreds of black leather held together with tarnished studs. Its chest was wound with a makeshift bandage soaked with blood and filth, and the right arm was cinched tightly to the rib cage by a belt.

"I am Colonel Ivan Vesensky of FSE Intelligence," the figure croaked in a parody of a human voice. It dropped to its knees in the soft red dirt by the roadside. "Must report—must report to Chairman Maximov—"

It collapsed at their feet, and lay still.

All Pan books are available at your local bookshop or newsagent, or can be ordered direct from the publisher. Indicate the number of copies required and fill in the form below.

Send to: **CS Department, Pan Books Ltd., P.O. Box 40,
             Basingstoke, Hants.   RG21 2YT.**

or phone: 0256 469551 (Ansaphone), quoting title, author
             and Credit Card number.

Please enclose a remittance* to the value of the cover price plus: 60p for the first book plus 30p per copy for each additional book ordered to a maximum charge of £2.40 to cover postage and packing.

*Payment may be made in sterling by UK personal cheque, postal order, sterling draft or international money order, made payable to Pan Books Ltd.

Alternatively by Barclaycard/Access:

Card No.

Signature:

Applicable only in the UK and Republic of Ireland.

While every effort is made to keep prices low, it is sometimes necessary to increase prices at short notice. Pan Books reserve the right to show on covers and charge new retail prices which may differ from those advertised in the text or elsewhere.

NAME AND ADDRESS IN BLOCK LETTERS PLEASE:

....

Name ——————————————————————————————

Address ——————————————————————————————

——————————————————————————————————

——————————————————————————————————

——————————————————————————————————

3/87